A Family Matter

A Family Matter

by Chris Laing

Seraphim
EDITIONS

The publisher gratefully acknowledges the financial assistance of the Canada Council for the Arts and the Ontario Arts Council.

Library and Archives Canada Cataloguing in Publication

Laing, Chris, 1936-, author
    A family matter / by Chris Laing.

(A Max Dexter mystery)
ISBN 978-1-927079-45-4 (softcover)

    I. Title. II. Series: Laing, Chris, 1936 . Max Dexter mystery

PS8623.A395F35 2017   C813'.6   C2017-900919-2

Editor: Bernadette Rule
Author Photo: Michèle LaRose
Cover and book design: Julie McNeill, McNeill Design Arts
Hamilton street scene courtesy of Janet Forjan, www.hamiltonpostcards.com

Published in 2017 by
Seraphim Editions
4456 Park Street
Niagara Falls, ON
L2E 2P6

Printed and bound in Canada

For Michèle

"My Sugar is so Refined"

CHAPTER ONE

THE LAST PERSON I WANTED to see again was my mother.

But she turned up anyway.

A two-bit Mafia mug by the name of Bernie Fiore called me at my office. "Meet me at the Tiv at 3:30," he said. "Upstairs in the loges, first row, beside the wall."

"What the hell, Bernie? I work for a living – no time for movies in the middle of the day."

"I can't talk no more." His voice a whisper now, "Just meet me there, Max. It's about your mother." Then he fumbled with the receiver and hung it up like a guy with ten thumbs.

I slumped in my chair, still clutching the phone, the dial tone a swarm of bees in my ear. My palm felt clammy as I plunked the receiver back on its cradle, my mind spinning.

How could it be about my mother? Was she back in Hamilton after all these years? And even more disturbing – why in hell would Bernie Fiore know a damn thing about her?

I stood at my office window, staring at the brick wall next door, as a slender, dark-haired woman slunk from the shadows of my mind. She was sheathed in a silvery dress shimmering with sequins and was smoking a cigarette in an ivory holder.

My father was spread-eagled in his armchair beside the radio; his Hamilton Police jacket, reeking of cigar smoke, was flung across the back of the sofa, his suspenders drooped at half-mast over his beer gut, and another quart bottle of Dow Ale was clamped in his massive right fist.

He sneered in her direction. "On the town again tonight?"

She turned to face him and shot back, "On the booze again tonight?"

He swallowed another long gulp, then waved the bottle toward her as though he were shooing a fly. "Good riddance."

At the honk of a car horn she draped a lacy shawl over her arm and sashayed toward the door as she snapped over her shoulder, "Same to you, Buster."

She didn't say a word to me – didn't seem to notice I was there, a skinny little kid with tears in his eyes, watching her disappear.

That was in 1923, what some folks called the Roaring Twenties. And I was seven years old when my mother roared out of my life. Now, a week before Christmas in 1947, I'd neither seen nor heard from her since.

She'd disappeared soon after my father was gunned down during a police raid on one of Rocco Perri's bootlegging joints along the Beach Strip. Years later, I heard a rumour that she had run off with one of Rocco's gunmen and that she might even be connected to the Mob somewhere in Florida. But I never knew for sure.

Isabel bustled into my office with a cheery "Morning, Max," rousing me from my dismal reverie. "You okay? You look like you've seen a ghost."

I pulled myself together, sat up straight in my chair and gave myself a quick head-rub. "I'm a bit dozy today. Must be the weather." I glanced toward the window – it wasn't the weather. Sunlight flooded in, reflecting off the powdery snow that had dusted the city overnight.

Iz drew up a chair and reached for my hand. "Something's going on, Max. Tell me."

Her green eyes held mine and wouldn't let go. My natural inclination to keep myself buttoned up didn't stand a ghost of a chance. "Thinking about old times," I half-confessed, and picked up a file folder from my in-basket. "Now, this new Nelligan case looks interesting. Think we could handle the surveillance on our own?"

She reached across the desk, plucked the folder from my hand and tossed it aside like a soiled Kleenex. "Oh, phooey, Max, the Nelligan case can wait. Now what about these 'old times'?"

She grasped my hand and squeezed, her vivid green eyes flashing.

Isabel O'Brien.

The stunning red-haired woman who'd been keeping me off balance since she'd joined Max Dexter Associates last summer to train with me as a private investigator. Six months later, I still hadn't learned to adjust to her straight-for-the-heart delivery. Does any man truly admit that he's met his match? That a woman – especially a woman as clever as Isabel – is almost as smart as he is? I checked myself. Forget about 'almost'. She was sharper than a fistful of carpet tacks.

"It's about my mother," I said, parroting Bernie's phrase. "Remember I told you she left Hamilton after my father was killed back in the twenties?"

She didn't speak, waiting for the other shoe to drop.

"I just got a call from Bernie Fiore, a young guy from the old neighbourhood. Last I heard, he was an enforcer with the Dominic Tedesco crime family. He says he wants to talk to me about her."

"She's back in town?"

"Bernie didn't say. I don't know why she'd come back now. And I don't think I'd want to meet her if she did."

Isabel stood and stepped behind me, placing both her hands on my shoulders. Her subtle fragrance teased me as she massaged the tightened muscles in my neck.

I leaned back in my chair. "Mmm – don't stop."

"If she is in town then you should see her, Max. Every mother must feel something for her only child. Even after all these years."

I reached back and held her arm. Then I gave her a big smile and changed the subject again. This time she followed my lead.

After lunch I stepped out onto King Street, relieved to see the sun had melted the light overnight snow. Wintry weather wasn't the best time of year for a war vet making do with a shrapnel wound that buggered up his right knee. I limped to the nearby Capitol Theatre where I spotted my friend Bob seated aboard his wheeled dolly.

He looked up when I approached, a grin on his clean-shaven face. "Hey there, Sarge, how goes the battle?"

"Okey-dokey. How's business here?"

In front of him on the sidewalk, he'd spread a small rubber mat where his pencils were lined up like toy soldiers ready for inspection. Bob had lost both legs at Dieppe but that didn't stop him from scooting himself around the downtown streets, setting up shop at the busiest spots. Bob extended his right hand. When I shook it, I noticed the tips of the thumb and first two fingers of his woolen glove had been snipped off: I guessed so he could handle his pencils better and make change.

"Business is always good at Christmastime, Sarge. What's up?"

I chuckled to myself. I wasn't a sergeant in the military police anymore, but some of my fellow vets still liked to call me Sarge.

"I'm meeting a guy at the Tivoli – about 1530. Think you could set up there? Keep an eye open for me?"

"Sure. Who're you meeting?"

"Bernie Fiore. Know him?"

He nodded then pushed back his army field cap as it tipped forward. "Yeah, I see him around quite a bit. A young mob guy: I think they've got him on collections – the old protection racket. He hangs out at that pool room down near the corner of Cannon and James. But dumber than a pile of bricks. His brother got all the brains in that family."

I smiled at his description. Bernie's older brother Nick had been a few years ahead of me at Central Collegiate: a hard-nosed lineman on the football team and that kept him in shape for his weekend job hustling booze for the Rocco Perri gang. And after Rocco's sudden disappearance – some said at the bottom of Hamilton Harbour – Nick was playing full-time on the Dominic Tedesco team.

"I'll be there, Sarge. You can count on me."

CHAPTER TWO

MID-AFTERNOON, I SLIPPED INTO MY overcoat and grabbed my grey fedora from on top of the filing cabinet by the door. When I left my office I had to jostle with an army of Christmas shoppers surging along King Street and filling the shops. Road traffic was also heavy – two Belt Line streetcars added to the din, one heading west, the other going east, their bells clanging at pedestrians bold enough to cross in mid-block. So I cut over to King William to avoid the clamour, then up to James Street North.

I spotted Bob in the wide entranceway of the Tivoli Theatre; he'd stationed himself beside a life-sized poster that shouted: **NOW PLAYING – *The Big Sleep*.** A cigarette dangled from Bogey's lips as he gawked at Lauren Bacall in a slinky dress, who skewered him with a sultry look. A tagline across the poster caught my eye: **The type of man she hated ... was the type she wanted.**

Bob wore what looked like a cut-down Army great-coat, probably remodelled for him by his sister Aggie with whom he lived nearby. His pencils were on parade as before and he glanced up at me as I approached. "Pencil, Mister?"

"Yeah, sure." I pretended to survey his display while a middle-aged couple paused nearby to read the movie ads. The woman was cooing over a poster of Princess Elizabeth and her new hubby. "Just look at this, Dearie" and she tugged on her husband's sleeve. "*Motion Pictures of the Royal Wedding* – in Technicolor."

They moved away and I turned back to Bob. "I'll take one of those HBs." I removed my gloves and dug out my wallet. Then I slipped him a couple of bucks for helping me out.

The money disappeared into his coat pocket in a sleight of hand motion that Blackstone the Magician might have envied, then he lowered his voice. "Bernie went in five minutes ago. Alone." He selected a pencil and made a production of presenting it to me with a flourish and raised his voice for the benefit of a couple of other bystanders who might've been keeping an eye on the lobby. "Thanks, Mister, and a Merry Christmas to you."

I ponied up two bits for a matinée ticket and crossed the lobby toward the wide staircase to the right of the snack bar where the carnival odour of popping corn had attracted a couple of old-timers.

At the top of the stairs I paused, allowing my eyes to adjust to the semi-darkness. On the screen Bacall was giving Bogey some lip, the kind of smart-ass dialogue I liked: "So you're a private detective," she said. "I didn't know they existed, except in books, or else they were greasy little men snooping around hotel corridors." That remark gave me pause: was Max Dexter like his fictional idol, Philip Marlowe, up there in black and white? Or was he that sleazy little snooper meeting a Mob guy on the sly in the gloom of the Tivoli Theatre?

I turned away from the screen and spotted Bernie right away – he was slouched beside the balcony wall in a short row of empty seats, munching on big handfuls of popcorn. I side-stepped down the row to join him. I hadn't seen him since I'd shipped overseas in '39. He was much bigger now – a brawny, brick shithouse of a guy. Bob had said he worked for the Mob as muscle, and he fitted that stereotype to a T: the kind of guy you'd avoid in an alley, dark or otherwise.

I shrugged out of my coat and when I sat down he withdrew his right hand from his greasy popcorn bag, wiped it along the side of his seat cushion and stretched it out for me to shake. I waved it away with a scowl. "Just tell me why we're here, Bernie. What's all this guff about my mother?"

He yanked his hand back, a half-assed sneer on his mug. "It ain't guff. It's the straight goods." His chin tilted up. "And they call me *Bernardo* now."

He rubbed his hands along his thighs, his bag of popcorn now wedged between his knees.

I nudged his arm. "I'm waiting, Bernie ... *excuse me*, Bernardo."

"Yeah, well, don't rush me. I'm thinking of a trade."

I stood up and leaned toward him. "See you around, Bud."

Bernie jumped to his feet. "Wait, Max!" He spoke a little too loudly and I saw a few heads in the seats below us turn upward. Someone made a shushing noise. Bernie sat down and lowered his voice. "I need your help with my brother."

Reluctantly, I sat down too. "You mean Nick? What's his problem?"

"He's in the clink. Barton Street." He leaned in closer, spraying me with his popcorn breath. "And he needs your help to get him out."

"What? Even if I could do that, why the hell should I?"

"That's the trade I was talking about," his head now bobbing like a kid's toy. "You agree to help Nick and I'll tell you about your mother meeting with Mr. Tedesco."

Whammo! Like walking into a brick wall.

So she *was* here. And with Tedesco, to boot.

I slowed my breathing and tried to put the brakes on my runaway thoughts. "When did she arrive?"

"Few days ago, I think. But I ain't saying no more unless you agree to help Nick."

"This is *his* idea?"

"Well ... sort of. Nick told me you used to be a copper. We all talked about it after you shot Mr. Tedesco's driver a couple months ago."

I allowed myself a small smile of satisfaction, imagining Tedesco and his thugs sitting around in their social club on Cannon Street, puffing on their stogies and discussing what to do about that goddamn private dick who had the nerve to fight back when threatened. So far Tedesco hadn't retaliated and I began to wonder if Bernie's presence here in the Tivoli might be the opening act in some sort of payback scheme to even the score with Max Dexter. But why would he send a slow-on-the-draw guy like Bernie Fiore?

Because sometime it was smart to seem stupid?

I shrugged those questions away – unanswered. "So Nick asked you to call me? To see what I could do for him?"

"Well ... he told me about your mother coming to town. So I thought, maybe if I told you about it, you know, you'd agree to help Nick."

"Did Tedesco tell you to contact me?"

"Oh, jeez, no." He leaned in closer, his eyes wide and jittery. "If he knew I was talking to you he'd shit a brick. And you ain't telling him, are you, Max?"

I shook my head – the poor bugger. It must have been a giant step for him to go behind Tedesco's back to talk with me. Bob was right about Bernie and that pile of bricks. But what could *I* do about his brother?

I shrugged his hand from my arm. "What's Nick been charged with?"

"Murder."

That got my attention.

"He was meeting some guy in the west end last week. And the guy died somehow."

Holy hell. I was gaping at him now. "You talking about that murder at Paddy Greene's?"

"Well, yeah. You heard about it, eh?"

Everybody had heard about it. The newspapers and the radio couldn't stop talking about it. For the newshounds it was like the Evelyn Dick case all over again. Because the "some guy" Bernie referred to was Controller George Harris, chairman of the city's Planning Committee. And the "somehow" was as a result of having his throat slit, almost to the point of decapitation. His body had been dumped in the ravine behind Paddy Greene's Tavern on Main Street West and, according to *The Hamilton Spectator*, the estimated time of the killing was two or three days before. Estimated, because the body had been "extensively interfered with by wild animals." All in all, I thought that was quite harsh treatment, even for a politician.

I swiveled in my seat to look at Bernie face-on. "Yeah, I heard about it. Did Nick kill that guy?"

"Hell, no. He told me he didn't. That's why you have to help him."

"But how can you be so sure it wasn't him?"

My question seemed to baffle him, his mouth open but no words coming out.

I waited.

"Nick never lies to me. He said that him and Sal Angotti were meeting this guy at Paddy Greene's. Then something must've happened 'cause the guy ended up dead."

"So you're saying this Sal guy killed him."

"Don't know. But Nick said Sal went kinda crazy."

"Then why's Nick in jail and not Sal?"

He gave me that puzzled look again, as though the answer was obvious. "Well, the cops got the wrong guy, didn't they?"

"Maybe they did, but I don't see what I can do about it. Tedesco's lawyers will represent Nick in court and if they make a good case they could get him off."

"Yeah, but you know what them damn lawyers are like. They don't give a damn if Nick goes to jail – or even gets the noose. That's why I'm coming to you, Max." He began fidgeting again, glancing around the theatre. Something must've caught his eye that spooked him because he jumped out of his seat, his popcorn cascading onto the floor. And he bent toward me as he squeezed past. "Wait a few minutes before you leave, Max. No offence but I don't want nobody to see me talking to you."

I took a quick look around at the handful of patrons up here but none seemed interested in us. Bernie paused in the aisle for a few seconds, brushing the popcorn from his coat, the kernels bouncing off his shoes – a spiffy pair of black and white wingtips that seemed to glow in the hooded light illuminating the carpeted stairs.

After he left I stretched out my legs and stared at the screen, trying to make sense of our meeting. Bogie and Bacall were still sparring with each other, not affected in the least by what Bernie had told me.

But what had I really learned about my mother's arrival in Hamilton, apparently to meet with Tedesco? Bugger-all. Bernie's information could fit neatly into a thimble, with room left over. She was here. They were meeting.

And what had he told me about Nick's involvement in the murder of that politician? Also bugger-all. Nick met the chairman. He died. Nick didn't do it. It must've been the other guy.

It made me wonder if Bernie had picked up a few pointers from the "Bullshit Baffles Brains" chapter in the *Gangsters' Handbook*.

I closed my eyes for a moment, wondering how my life could have changed so quickly. Just last night Isabel and I were snuggled together in her living room, sipping hot toddies, Nat King Cole on the radio serenading us with "... *chestnuts roasting on an open fire* ..." as we tip-toed around the possibility of sharing a life together. Iz had recovered well from her injuries in October, when one of Tedesco's thugs had run her off the road. She was fortunate to escape with only a broken ankle. And I'd gotten over my civilian's heebie-jeebies after I was forced to shoot one of his men who had tried to kill me. In addition, Max Dexter Associates was doing better with a number of new accounts and the prospect of breaking even for the year.

But now, along comes Bernie Fiore saying my mother was back in town and bringing with her the possibility of another unwanted encounter with Dominic Tedesco. I wondered what I'd done to deserve this bounty. I think it was some guy in the Bible who said, "Sometimes life ain't fair."

I pulled myself together, picked up my hat and coat from the seat beside me and made my way downstairs where I watched Bob delivering his sales pitch to an old guy with one of those wiener dogs on a leash. I didn't think it was actually unpatriotic to own a German dog but still, so soon after the war ...

I hung back a short distance until Bob had finished with his customer. "Thanks for keeping watch this afternoon. Lots of business?"

"Not bad here, Sarge. But look at all the folks across the street." He was aiming his chin toward Eaton's department store which occupied the entire block from Merrick Street all the way up to City Hall. Shoppers were crowded in front of the

A Family Matter | 17

Christmas display windows and the brass revolving doors were in constant motion.

I turned back to Bob. "Did you see Bernie when he left?"

"Yeah, I watched his reflection in the glass surrounding the ticket booth so he wouldn't notice me. Then I wheeled onto the sidewalk and saw him heading north. He kept looking around like he was afraid somebody might be keeping an eye on him. But the dumb cluck didn't even notice the two guys who stepped out of Peace's Cigar Store and tailed him."

I peered down at him, admiring his observation skills and thinking that he might've been a better military copper than an infantryman. "What did they look like, these followers? Mob guys or plainclothes police?"

"Oh, they were gangsters for sure. Cops ain't sharp dressers like those Mob mutts."

I chuckled as I passed him the pencil he'd sold me. "Here. I've got a lifetime supply of these things. Thanks again for your help."

He wheeled away, heading up James Street, waving his arm over his head without looking back at me. I glanced in the direction Bernie had taken – the two guys tailing him no longer in sight. I couldn't help feeling a pang of pity for him; he seemed so certain he'd been flying under the Mob's radar by meeting me here in the darkness of the Tivoli Theatre. Too damn bad he wasn't as smart as those wingtips he wore on his big feet.

CHAPTER THREE

I CROSSED OVER JAMES STREET to Eaton's and joined a group of shoppers gawking at a window display of women's jewellery arrayed beneath a Christmas tree. A Santa mannequin appeared to be arranging these baubles; beside him a spangled banner proclaimed, *Santa knows what women wish for.* My eye was drawn to the diamond engagement rings and I wondered if Santa knew what Isabel wished for. I hadn't gotten her a Christmas present yet but a ring like that could change a guy's life.

I kept walking.

When I got back to the office Isabel peppered me with questions before I got my hat and coat off.

"Hold your horses, Iz. Let's go in and sit down."

At my desk, I rested my leg across an opened drawer, stretched back in my chair and let out a long breath as the dull ache in my right knee subsided.

Iz was watching this performance with a wry smile and I half-expected her to comment upon my manly ability to tolerate pain. Instead, she said, "Your mother. Tell me everything."

So much for half-expectations.

"Bernie says she's back in town. Meeting with Tedesco."

"But why? What's she up to? And why would she be meeting with criminals? I don't understand."

I held up my hand, waiting for her to run out of steam. "Scout's honour, Iz. I don't know much about her. Years ago I'd heard that she might be connected with the Mob in Florida but nothing more than that. Bernie wanted my help to get his brother out of jail in exchange for info about my mother. But he came up short on both counts."

A frown crinkled her features as she thought about that. "But is she *really* here? Maybe he was lying to you."

"Not Bernie, it's not his style. His job is to put the squeeze on the Mob's slow-paying customers. Period."

"But he was smart enough to come to you for help with his brother. And he used your mother as bait – and that's not so dumb."

She was right, as usual. "That occurred to me too. But he was so worried about his brother, well, I was convinced he was being straight with me. And he was desperate enough to risk going behind Tedesco's back to meet with me."

Her eyes held mine and I couldn't tell whether she thought I was on the right track or not. "Tell me about his brother," she said.

"His name's Nick. He's older than Bernie and he's been a gang member since he was in high school. Now he's in the Barton Street Jail – arrested for the murder of that Board of Control member last week."

"Holy Doodle, Max – that was such a gruesome crime. Why would Bernie think you'd want to help *him*?"

"Like I said, he's desperate and he can hardly go to the police for help. He remembers me from the old neighbourhood and he knows that I'm a detective now, so ..."

She reached across the desk, placing her hand on mine. "You're such a soft touch, Max. It's one of your best qualities." Now she was squeezing my hand. "But sometimes it can get you into trouble."

I saw a flicker of fear in her eyes. She knew first-hand how dangerous it could be to rub up against the Mob. And if you were lucky, you might only land up in St. Joe's emergency ward instead of the morgue.

"I'm worried that you might be in danger again, Max. I want us to be together for a long time." She withdrew her hand and leaned back in her chair. "But I still think it's important that you see your mother." Her voice with some spine in it now. "And if that means we might be involved with Tedesco and Company again, then I'll be with you all the way."

I was sitting on that proverbial fence: a happily-ever-after life with Isabel on one side – and a congregation of alligators snapping at my ass on the other.

CHAPTER FOUR

IT WAS CLOSING TIME AND I was looking out my third floor window at the traffic snaking along King Street; most of the cars had their lights on as the shortest day in the year approached. The downtown stores were decked out in seasonal trappings but I'd read in *The Hamilton Spectator* that Ontario Hydro had banned all outdoor decorative lighting, even in display windows, in order to conserve electricity for industrial use. It made sense, I supposed, because The Steel Company, Dofasco, Westinghouse, all those big factories were able to increase production now that the labour force had swelled with the return of the veterans from overseas. But I missed seeing the trees in Gore Park dressed in their traditional glow of Christmas lights.

Isabel was wearing her long red coat with the Persian lamb collar when she joined me at the window. She held a pair of black leather gloves in her left hand. "Looks strange without the trees lit up, doesn't it?"

"Sure does."

As I turned from the window I noticed our secretary, Phyllis, waiting in the doorway. No fur collar on her coat, but she wore a matching green hat with a sprig of ivy pinned to it. And on her lapel a tiny pair of white figure skates dangled from a silver clip. "Isabel and I are off to do some Christmas shopping, Max. The stores are on extended hours so you're welcome to join us."

I grinned at Phyllis. She was Hamilton's biggest fan of Barbara Ann Scott – Canadian figure skating champion and Canada's best hope, so Phyllis said, for a gold medal at the Olympic Games in Switzerland in February. A picture of "Canada's Sweetheart" was taped to the filing cabinet beside her desk and she kept a

scrapbook filled with newspaper and magazine clippings chroni-
cling the young skater's rise to fame.

"Don't tell me," I said. "You're shopping for a pair of Barbara
Ann skates."

She blushed. "Maybe Santa will bring me a pair. But what
about it, Max? Come shopping with us – it'll be fun."

I caught the fleeting smirk on Isabel's face. "Maybe next
time," I said. "But thanks for asking."

After they'd gone, I returned to my desk and called Frank Russo
at the Central Police Station. "How about a beer at Duffy's?"

"I thought you were barred from that joint?"

"A barrel of monkeys, that's what you are, Frank."

His voice became muffled as he covered his phone to speak
to someone in his office. He was back a moment later, "See you
there in 15 minutes."

As I was locking my office door I heard the bing of the elevator
bell and hiked down the hallway on the double. The doors were
about to close after a tall guy in a black coat got out and was
heading for the offices at the far end of the hallway. He wore a
pair of galoshes with the buckles undone and they jangled like a
pocketful of loose change as he hurried along.

"Hold that car," I called out and Tiny the operator stuck his
head out the door, waving me aboard. As I entered I caught a
whiff of Old Spice in the air; must've been from the guy who'd
just gotten off because Tiny wasn't a cologne kind of guy. And
neither was I.

"Looks like you've got a spring in your step, Sarge." He slid
the doors shut, cranked the handle to put the elevator in gear
then turned toward me with a smirk on his pixie face. "Must be
meeting someone special, eh?"

"Not who you think. It's Frank Russo – remember him from
your time in the RHLI?"

"Yeah, a good guy. A buddy of mine was in his platoon
overseas."

Tiny stopped the elevator on the main floor and was searching his pockets for something. "Hang on, Sarge. Some guy came by and passed me a note for you."

He slipped me a small piece of grey cardboard folded in half – it looked like it had been snipped off one of those dividers you find in a box of Muffets cereal. Scrawled on it was, *Forgot to give you this*, and a phone number. It was signed, *B*.

"Who dropped this off?"

"I didn't know the guy. Some big palooka, all dressed up like Fred Astaire, but he wouldn't give me his name."

I supposed it was Bernie Fiore's idea of covering his backside. And I couldn't blame him for trying.

Wispy snowflakes danced in the air as I stepped onto King Street; a gusty wind had passersby holding onto their hats and I turned up my coat collar. My office was in the building beside *The Hamilton Spectator* and I joined a small knot of people scanning the leading news stories that the newspaper posted in its large front windows. A picture of a gigantic Christmas tree in downtown New York with its lights aglow was splashed across the first page. But a headline on the following page evoked a darker image, *"Arabs fighting Brits in Palestine against the Holy Land partition."* It made me wonder if the conflict between the Arabs and the Jews would ever be settled.

Duffy's Tavern was in the next block. I breezed through the doorway and brushed the snowflakes from my coat with my gloves. I spotted Frank at a table away from the crowded bar where the regulars laughed and gossiped in raised voices. A tree decorated with tiny coloured lights blinked beside the juke box – Bing Crosby crooning, "I'm Dreaming of a White Christmas" – a nice tune but since its release in 1942, you heard it everywhere at this time of year, and I mean *everywhere*.

Liam shot me a big salute from behind the bar and pointed toward Frank's table where I dumped my coat and hat on an empty chair and shook his hand before I plunked myself down. Two bottles of Peller's Ale sat in front of him and he slid one toward me with the middle finger of his right hand.

We clinked bottles and glugged some beer. "Haven't seen you for a week or so, Maxie. Been keeping out of trouble?"

"One man's trouble is another man's recreation, as Al Capone used to say."

He leaned forward to deliver a light punch to my arm then slouched back in his chair. "Doesn't surprise me you're a fan of Capone's. The way you thumb your nose at the law."

"Not me, Frank. I'm as law-abiding as the next guy."

"That's not sayin' much. Not in this town."

I laughed at his joke that wasn't a joke and we drank our beer as Bing Crosby now gave way to Johnny Mercer and the Pied Pipers singing "Winter Wonderland".

The spicy aroma of corned beef teased my nostrils and I envied the guy two tables away as he popped a French fry into his mouth then reached for his mile-high sandwich. "You got time to eat, Frank? Or something else planned?"

He waved my suggestion away. "Angie and I are going to the neighbours' for dinner tonight and the guy's wife makes the world's best *Stracotto al Chianti* so there's no way I'm going to miss that."

"I don't know that dish."

"It's beef braised in a wine sauce." He bunched the fingers of his right hand together and touched them to his lips. "*Magnifico*."

Then he leaned forward and lowered his voice. "You sounded serious on the phone. So what's on your mind?"

His black eyes held mine in their grip, just like the old days. After my father was killed and my mother left town, Frank's family, who lived in the apartment above us, had taken me in to live with them. That's when Frank became my big brother, a relationship that continued to this day. I took a deep breath, then let it out slowly. "My mother's back in town."

"What?" That news seemed to hit him like a punch in the gut. "After twenty-some years? Who the hell told you that?"

"Bernie Fiore."

"Shee-it," he turned up his nose and made a fanning motion with his hand as though he were shooing away a nasty smell. "That dumb bugger doesn't know his ass from his elbow. How would he know anything about her?"

"He says she's meeting with Tedesco."

A scowl now on his Calabrian features, accentuated by his five-o'clock shadow. "Even if that's true, why would he risk telling you about Mob business? If Tedesco found out, he'd eat Bernie alive."

"I know. But he thinks he's making a trade with me. He tells me about my mother and I'm supposed to help him get his brother out of jail."

Frank tipped his head back and guzzled a long swig of beer, then set the bottle down in its condensation ring. "Let me guess." He covered his mouth and burped. "Bernie told you his brother didn't do it. Nick's in jail for somebody else's crime – he was in Montreal at the time. Hang on – better still, he was at his dying mother's bedside. And he's got five witnesses who'll swear to it."

I gave him a theatrical sigh, waiting for him to finish his routine.

"Bernie knows you and I are friends because we all grew up in the same North End neighbourhood. And he gets this bright idea to make up a story about your mother so you'll come to me for help to get his brother out of jail." He pushed his beer aside and leaned closer. "A crazy idea, isn't it? And that's just the kind of dumb-ass plan Bernie would come up with."

His chin was jutting out, challenging me. "What about it? I'm right, eh?" Then he sat back, picked up his beer and I saw that familiar smug expression on his puss which said, *You don't know shit from shinola.*

That look – he was wearing it when he came to my rescue during schoolyard fights, and when he forged his mother's signature on my not-so-good report cards. And especially when I signed up with the RCMP right out of high school in 1934 instead of joining him on the Hamilton Police Force.

I stood up and waved at Liam and when I got his attention I held up two fingers for another round; then I pointed to the guy two tables away and mimed eating a sandwich and held up one finger. I waited for him to nod his head. Then I scooted my chair closer to Frank's. "You could be right about Bernie but I don't think so. He was jumpy as hell when I met him this afternoon, so scared he might be seen with me that we met in the balcony at the Tivoli. But when he left the theatre a couple of torpedoes slipped out of Peace's Cigar Store and tailed him. Something's going on, Frank, and I don't think Bernie's making it up."

"What did he say about your mother?"

"Not much. Just what I told you."

He shook his head again. "She left town when you were just a kid, so why would you want anything to do with her now?"

Before I could reply he shifted forward in his chair and lowered his voice. "Look, you've heard the same story I have that she's part of the Tataglia Mob down there in Florida. If Bernie's right and she really is here, it's got to be on Mob business. So if I were in your shoes I'd stay the hell away from her."

I shrugged his arm off my shoulder and gazed toward the revelers at the bar, envying their Christmas mood. Of course, he was probably right about my mother. And I was almost certain that Bernie's offer of information about her was just a desperate attempt to save his brother's ass. But couldn't there still be some sort of mother-son bond, as Isabel had suggested? Shit – I thought I'd gotten over this confusion years ago.

Liam arrived at the table with a tray: two more Pellers and a big fat corned beef on rye for me. He reached for the empties and said, "You guys just get back from a funeral? Cheer up; it's the holiday season, in case you haven't noticed."

Frank looked up at him. "I'm advising Max on his love life." He pointed a thick finger at me. "You can see how crappy it is."

When Liam left, I sprinkled some salt and a dash of vinegar on the fries then slid the plate between us. "Tell me about that murder at Paddy Greene's, Frank. Are you sure Nick Fiore's your man?"

For a few seconds I thought he might launch into his usual song and dance about sharing confidential police business with mere civilians. But he surprised me. "Looks like he's guilty, but I'm not certain yet." He picked up a sizzling French fry in his finger-tips and blew on it. "The City Planning Committee was considering an application for a big apartment complex funded by a holding company controlled by Tedesco. And get this –" he was jabbing the French fry at me like a pointer. "The Chairman intended to reject it. Sounds like a motive to get rid of him, eh?"

"Maybe. But it might've been just a warning that went off the rails." I was thinking about Bernie's remark that the police got the wrong guy.

"What makes you say that? Something Bernie told you?"

"Yeah. He said Nick and Sal Angotti met up with the Chairman and –"

"Hang on a minute." Frank leaned closer and lowered his voice, "You sure he said Sal Angotti?"

I nodded and took another juicy bite of my sandwich and chewed on it while I waited for him to continue.

"Angotti was a member of the Magaddino crew in Buffalo until he dropped out of circulation a few months ago. Cops down there thought he was deep-sixed because he'd become too hard to control and was bringing heat on the family. So it's interesting that he's shown up here. Your pal Tedesco must be desperate if has to hire a loose cannon like Angotti."

My "pal" Tedesco. Sure as hell, he was no pal of mine. Just a few months ago his thugs had delivered a painful message to Isabel and me when we came too close to exposing his involvement in the murders of two Hamilton businessmen.

Frank wiped his fingers with a paper napkin. "You were telling me what Bernie said about his brother."

"Nick told him that he didn't kill that councillor."

He bellowed a guffaw and a young couple at a nearby table looked our way. Then he lowered his voice. "And that's Bernie's proof that Nick didn't do it? Because he said so?"

"I asked him if Sal Angotti did it."

"And?"

"He didn't know."

Frank leaned back in his chair and sighed. "Dammit, Max, everybody knows that Bernie's a dumbbell. But it's news if Salvatore Angotti's in town. And if Bernie actually saw your mother and Tedesco together … "

I cut him off. "Then something big might be –"

"Yeah," and he reached over and snatched the last French fry off my plate.

CHAPTER FIVE

NEXT MORNING, I AWOKE SHIVERING; my sheet and blanket lay in a tangled heap on the floor. I glanced at my alarm clock – 0630. A stiff wind rattled the frosted panes in my bedroom window as I groped my way to the bathroom in the half-light. I scoured my face with an ice-cold wash cloth, trying to scrub away images from my nightmare of my mother and Tedesco, their heads together, refining their plot to seize control of the city's Planning Department now that the chairman was out of the way.

In the kitchen, a chilly draft seeped from the crack around the back door. I clicked on the mantle radio and set the coffee pot on the stove to percolate. The CHML weather guy said it would be cloudy, cold and breezy, maybe a few flurries.

Then Vic Copps rattled off the overnight NHL scores followed by his "editorial" comment. "With only seven weeks remaining before the first puck is dropped at the Olympic Games in St. Moritz," he said, "the controversy about the team chosen to represent Canada rages on. Some folks say the middle-aged men on the RCAF Flyers squad won't be able to cut the mustard. And now the Canadian Amateur Hockey Association plans to supply players to bolster the team after its 7–0 loss to the McGill University Redmen." My brain was too foggy to follow Vic's report so I snapped off the radio.

I poured a cup of Maxwell House and opened the ice-box only to find I was out of milk. It was probably too early for the Royal Oak Dairy guy, but I checked anyway. When I stepped onto the back porch, a frigid gust of wind whipped open my pajama top and I clutched it closed with my left hand as I lifted the lid of the milkbox with my right. There was my empty bottle, dammit, the milk ticket still stuck in its neck.

A narrow shaft of light from the kitchen door fell across a shape beside the milkbox. It looked like a pile of old clothes. So I stepped toward the door and kicked it open to cast more light out here.

I was right about the clothes. But, they were worn by a corpse.

A man's body had been dumped in a ghastly heap on my back stoop. It was facing away from me, the hair matted with dried blood. One arm was tucked beneath him, the other was bent at an awkward angle, his shirt sleeve dangling loose, missing its cuff link. His grey pants were twisted on his legs, the crotch soaked through. I recognized his shoes right away – black and white wingtips, the toe caps now scuffed and ruined. When I last saw them they were spit-shined and gleaming in the balcony of the Tivoli Theatre.

I'd seen more than my share of dead bodies, but you never get used to that electric jolt that sizzles up your spine, trying to paralyze you. I drew in a deep breath and knelt on my good knee to move the body onto its side; Bernie Fiore looked straight through me with that glassy-eyed dead-man's stare, a bloody crust behind his left ear where he'd been shot. Twice. His skin was the colour of January in Regina. The breath I'd been holding came out in a rush and I eased him back as I'd found him. That fecal stench of death engulfed me and I gripped the porch railing to steady myself as my stomach clenched.

For a horrifying moment I was back on that blood-drenched shore in Dieppe. Death and destruction boomed around me. Dead and dying comrades lay strewn along the slippery, rocky beach and bodies were bobbing face-down in the water. I closed my eyes and heard Bernie telling me in the Tivoli, "I don't want nobody to see me talking to you, Max."

I staggered back into the kitchen and slumped at the table. My gut heaved as another wave of nausea churned through me. A dead body on the battlefield was one thing – a corpse dumped on your own doorstep was quite another matter. Especially when it belonged to a guy I'd been meeting with yesterday.

It took me three tries to dial Frank's number.

"You're talking a mile a minute, Maxie. Now, take a couple of deep breaths and start over."

I was pacing between my front door and the kitchen while I awaited Frank's arrival, trying to calm the surge of emotions that still gripped me. He said he'd be here in half an hour, after he'd made arrangements with the coroner's guys to pick up the body. I quit my pacing to look out the living room window, the eastern sky brightening now as the neighbourhood was coming to life. I watched a guy across the street backing his '39 Plymouth coupé out of his driveway, heading off to work. A couple of young women hurried arm in arm toward King Street, huddled in their winter coats, their breath coming out in white puffs as they chatted. People leading ordinary lives, going about their daily business. God, how I envied them.

Frank pulled up in front of my ground-floor apartment on the corner of Emerald and Hunter Streets but remained in his car. I could see his cigarette smoke leaking from the driver's window that was opened a crack. A moment later a white van pulled in behind him, two guys in the cab. The driver got out, his white uniform glistening in the early morning sunlight as he hustled forward to have a word with Frank. Then a police car arrived and a young guy with a flash camera jumped out of the passenger side and joined the huddle at the curb.

When I'd called Frank I described the scene on my back porch so he led the coroner's attendants and the police photographer directly there and they set to work. I watched through the window of my kitchen door as the camera's flash lit up Bernie's limp body in stark relief. Then Frank examined him in much the same way as I had done. Finally, he waved for the guys in white to load the body onto their stretcher and take it to their van.

By this time, a small group of neighbours had gathered to gawk and gossip on the sidewalk, attracted by the hubbub at my back door and the coroner's vehicle at the curb. I was jealous of them, too. They could just walk away.

I sat at my kitchen table, now wearing an old pair of pants and a wrinkled, dirty work-shirt I'd yanked out of the laundry basket. Frank had completed his inspection and left his men to finish up. He helped himself to a cup of coffee. "No milk yet," I told him. "Should be here soon."

He pulled up a chair beside me and set his cup on the table. "A tough thing to wake up to, Maxie. You handling it all right?"

I tried to nod but it came out as a shake of my head. "As well as I can. A big shock though – seeing Bernie like that."

"I can imagine. Two shots, back of the head. Looks like Tedesco's sending you a Christmas card and it has sweet Fanny Adams to do with 'Peace on Earth'. Now tell me the real story about Bernie Fiore."

I sat upright in my chair, looking him straight in the eye. "I know it's not much, but I've told you everything. And I'm convinced Bernie was on the square – he was just looking for help to spring his brother from jail."

He lifted his cup and blew across the surface of his coffee. Then he tried a small sip but set the cup down in a hurry. "Got a can of Carnation?

I made a face and shook my head.

He stepped to the sink and ran a little cold water into his cup. "Sounds as though you liked Bernie."

"Well, he wasn't a smart guy but he was loyal. I'll give him that."

Frank returned to the table. "Whether he intended it or not, Bernie's stuck you smack-dab in the middle of this business. But what do we know for sure? He met you at the Tiv and now he's dead. And we only have his word for it that your mother's back in town meeting with Tedesco. Likewise that Sal Angotti's here and might've killed that City Controller." He shook his head again. "Bernie was trying to get his brother out of jail and he probably made up this whole damn story about your mother just to get your help. You said it yourself – he wasn't a smart guy."

I was about to reply when I heard someone outside the kitchen door. I hustled across the room, peeked out the window, then opened the door. The milkman stood on the porch, gaping at the coroner's guys at the curb as they lifted the stretcher with Bernie's body and slid it into their van.

"Sonovabitch," he said. "Was that a dead body those guys were carrying?"

I had to tug the bottle of milk from his grasp. "Yeah, but it's all over now. You can read about it in tonight's paper." And I shut the door.

I got busy at the kitchen counter clearing away the dishes, keeping myself moving and trying not to think about Bernie's corpse. But even in death, his empty stare blamed me for not helping him. Had he been executed simply for meeting with me at that Bogart movie? That seemed far-fetched.

Frank was keeping an eye on me but didn't speak until I took a seat at the table.

"There's another way of looking at this," he said. Then he edged toward me and gripped my arm. "Supposing I'm right about Bernie – that he lied about your mother because he thought you'd want to see her and you'd be grateful to him for that info. Then he fed you all that crapola about Angotti in order to get his brother off the hook."

I mulled that over. "It's possible, I guess. But why was he killed? And why would anyone dump his body at my place?"

"Here's what I've been thinking. Maybe it's got nothing to do with your mother or Angotti. You told me Bernie was being followed, right? So maybe Tedesco was having him watched because he was skimming from his collections or some other damn thing. And in the beginning it wasn't connected to you. But when Bernie was seen meeting with Max Dexter, pain-in-the-ass private detective, Tedesco sees that as an opportunity; two birds with one stone, eh? He figures he'll get rid of the problem he's been having with Bernie and use his dead body to scare the shit out of you – to let you know he hasn't forgotten that you killed one of his guys a few months ago. And that maybe you'll be next on his to-do list if you don't butt out of his damn business."

I was staring at him while he was speaking and realized I'd been holding my breath. I swallowed several times and wiped the beads of sweat from my forehead with my shirt sleeve. "Is this supposed to make me feel better? My mother's not in town but Tedesco's lining me up in his sights?"

Frank added milk and sugar to his coffee as I spoke and then he drank it down in three gulps. He got to his feet, put on his overcoat and fished out his car keys. "Just a theory, Bud, but think about it. Meantime, I'll see if I can get a car stationed nearby – in case you have more visitors."

CHAPTER SIX

AFTER FRANK LEFT I CALLED my office and spoke with Isabel, explaining my delay this morning.

I listened to her breathing – a sharp gasp as I described finding Bernie's body. "Oh, my gosh, Max. A dead body at your back door? Are you all right? Do you want me to come over?"

"No, no. I'm feeling better now. But it was a big shock to see Bernie … like that. So I might be a little late this morning. "

There was a long pause on the line.

"Isabel? You still there?"

"I don't suppose you've considered taking the day off, have you, Max?" Her voice was firmer now. "For heaven's sake, finding a corpse on your doorstep must be a terrible shock to your system. You could take some time off to recharge your batteries. I wouldn't think less of you if you did."

Damn, I was hoping Isabel might not have realized the extent to which the discovery of Bernie's body had shaken me up. I swallowed hard and my face felt like it was on fire. Why was I having such trouble admitting my feelings to this woman who now meant everything to me?

"Maybe you're right, Iz. Maybe I'll take it easy today, stay home and clean up my apartment. So I'll see you tomorrow. Goodbye."

I replaced the receiver in a hurry, my mind filled with self-doubt, up to my knees in pity for poor old Max. Then I plopped into my comfy chair in the living room, put my feet up on the ottoman and tried to clear my mind.

Tried, but failed.

I couldn't dismiss Frank's theory – that Tedesco was using Bernie Fiore's body as a scare tactic, to remind me that my own body could be dumped just like Bernie's – anywhere and anytime he damn well pleased. But did I get Bernie killed by being seen with him? Or did Bernie bring about his own death? And ... was I next?

An insistent knocking on my front door interrupted those dark thoughts and I tucked my shirt into my pants as I peeked through the window before opening the door.

An eager young guy gripping a flash camera in his right hand tipped his fedora in my direction. "Morning, Mr. Dexter. I'm Pete Homulos from *The Spectator*. Hope you don't mind a few quick questions – I won't bother you for long."

I gave him my hard stare. "Thought you guys got everything you needed from the police and the coroner's people. Sorry, I've got nothing to add."

I tried to close the door but the reporter slid forward, wheedling his way inside. "Did you know the dead man at your back door? They're saying he was a gangster, is that right?"

"If he was then you know more than I do." I tried to reach for his arm and shove him toward the door but he side-stepped me and brought up his camera, the flash blinding me.

His coat-tail was still in my grasp as we grappled in the doorway and I stumbled forward, pushing him onto the step. I'd regained my eyesight and was able to grab his arm. "If that photo turns out, you can't use it without my permission." I had no idea if that was true but maybe he didn't either.

He shook himself loose and was bustling toward the street when he slowed and called back over his shoulder. "You gave me permission when you invited me into your apartment. Merry Christmas, Mister."

I was about to respond but caught myself. If I'd told him to go to hell, he'd probably use that in his story. You couldn't win with these birds. I watched him cross the street, jump into a rusty red Chevy and drive off. Then I noticed an unmarked black Ford parked a few doors down on Emerald Street, a wispy vapour trail leaking from its exhaust pipe, the guy in the driver's seat smoking a cigarette and tapping his fingers on the steering wheel.

Frank said he'd have a cop stationed nearby and I breathed a little easier seeing him there.

I slammed the front door and leaned my back against it, catching my breath. "Pushy buggers, those newshounds," I said aloud. Then I imagined my picture in tonight's paper. I hadn't had time to bathe and shave this morning or even comb my hair. I was wearing that old pair of pants I'd pulled out of the laundry and my dirty shirt hung loose after the struggle in the doorway. That photo would probably make me look like a drunken bum who was about to pass out in an alley behind some bootlegger's joint in the north end of town.

I took a deep breath and decided to wipe the slate clean and make a new start to the day. It couldn't be any worse than my first try. I peeled off my old duds as I headed for the bathroom.

I was buttoning a clean shirt when the phone rang. Another damn reporter, I thought, possibly my Uncle Scotty at the *Spec*. Or maybe it was Frank.

It was neither.

"It's Isabel, Max. Are you feeling any better? You seemed annoyed with me when we spoke earlier."

"I'm fine now. And I apologize for being abrupt with you before."

I heard a sigh on the line before she spoke. "I should know by now that when you feel under pressure you just grit your teeth and carry on. It's not a bad trait, Max, but sometimes it scares me. You're not Superman, you know. I still think it would do you a world of good to rest up for a day or two."

I was touched by her concern for me. She was right, of course; I'd always tried to handle a difficult situation head-on and damn the torpedoes – it was the only way I knew. But now, if I wanted to share a life with Isabel and even raise a family with her, maybe I'd have to be more selective with the cases I chose to work on.

I wanted Iz – hell, I desperately needed her in my life. But I couldn't resist that deep-seated urge that compelled me to fight against the injustices which surrounded us: those greedy businessmen exploiting their workers, the crooked politicians who lined their pockets with taxpayers' money, and especially those mobsters who routinely defied the law and maimed or killed any-one who stood in their way. The kind of people who left other people dead on the doorsteps of law-abiding citizens.

But was it possible to have both? I knew I had to try.

"I agree with you, Iz, I'm not Superman. Hell's bells, I doubt if I could leap a dog house in a single bound, let alone a tall build-ing. I'm going to take it easy today, as you suggested. And ... thanks for checking up on me."

At suppertime, after a long day of jittery nerves, I was opening a can of McGinty's Irish Stew when I heard a loud thwack as some-thing banged against my front door.

Alarm bells clanged in my head and my stomach muscles clamped tight. Tedesco wouldn't hit me again, would he? Not twice in one day.

I peeked out the living room window toward the porch.

Nobody in sight.

Standing to the side of the door, I turned the knob and kicked it open.

No one.

I scanned the street; the coast was clear.

Then I noticed the Home edition of *The Hamilton Spectator* lodged in a shrub beside the step and I figured the paperboy must have ricocheted it off the door. I let out the breath I'd been hold-ing. I didn't see the carrier nearby so I was denied the satisfaction of giving the kid hell. I recovered the newspaper, locked the door and sat at the kitchen table where I pushed the half-opened can of stew aside and unfolded the paper with some trepidation.

There it was on the front page: a four-column photo of a dazed man in rumpled clothes. His disheveled hair was long and shaggy, his unshaven face contorted in an angry scowl. And beneath the photo in bold type:

Local detective finds body instead of milk delivery

The story was short on details: a few facts about Bernie, his age, his address and an oblique reference to his possible occupation. "Mr. Fiore's brother, Niccolo, a long-time member of Hamilton's underworld, is currently in the Barton Street Jail, charged with the murder of Controller George Harris of this city."

Max Dexter was quoted as saying, "I have nothing to say."

Poop. This wasn't the kind of publicity my new business needed.

The telephone rang again. I pushed back my chair and crossed the room to where the phone hung on the wall. When I grabbed the receiver I heard Frank crowing, "Is that Mr. Photogenic?"

I groaned.

"That picture's a real humdinger, Maxie. I bet you could run for 'Hobo of the Year'."

"You're a true friend, Frank. Making me feel a whole lot better."

He cleared his throat in a series of short coughs; something he did when he felt uncertain or uneasy, and sometimes when he realized he was being a horse's ass. "You're right. I guess I shouldn't be laughing, but that photo's a lulu."

"You've got some news about Bernie's murder?"

"No, I just wanted to know how you're doing. You still sound a bit jumpy."

"Well, it's been that kind of day, hasn't it? It started out with a bang and didn't get any better. But thanks for sending that car around. I felt relieved when I saw the guy stationed down the street."

He paused a long moment. "Listen ... I wasn't able to send the car yet."

I swallowed the lump in my throat. "What the –?"

"Hang on. Don't get your knickers in a knot. I just spoke with the sergeant in charge of the Radio Room and he told me there'll be a guy out front in 20 minutes."

I held myself in check – that watcher I saw parked down the street hadn't made a move on me yet and I doubted he would in the next 20 minutes. So I shut my gob and didn't bitch about the delay; no point in jeopardizing the provision of a free bodyguard.

"That's swell, Frank. I should be okay until your man gets here."

I'd forgotten to turn the stove on and the bowls were all dirty, so I ate my stew cold from the pot. Isabel called again, and I reassured her with more confidence than I felt. The day wasn't going to get any better so I added the dirty pot and bowl to the pile in the sink and peeked through the front window for that police car, but didn't see it. I went to bed.

But before I slid under the covers, I retrieved my father's .32 Colt revolver from the closet and set it on the bedside table. It wouldn't hurt to be prepared in case uninvited visitors decided to pay me a late-night call.

When I closed my eyes I envisioned Dominic Tedesco smirking at my mother while he stood over the bloodied body of Bernie Fiore on my back porch. "Hamilton is my show," he told her, "and if you don't keep your goddamn kid from nosing into my business, he'll end up just like this dumb bugger."

CHAPTER SEVEN

I AWOKE TO THE ROYAL OAK DAIRY guy rattling his bottles in their metal carrier and for a few nerve-tingling seconds the image of Bernie Fiore's lifeless body held me in its grasp once more. I felt my way to the kitchen door and out to the milk-box – a quart of milk. No bodies. And judging by the milkman's footprints, about an inch of powdery snow had fallen overnight, which might've delayed him on his rounds this morning.

It was already 0830 as I slurped down my Grape-Nuts Flakes while standing at the sink. Last night hadn't been a night of rest – mean, muscle-bound kids from my old neighbourhood ganged up on me after school, chasing and beating me with baseball bats. Later, a couple of German soldiers took turns torturing me in a French farmhouse. Then Tedesco's troops dangled me from the Tivoli's marquee, using my body for target practice. And above this tableau my mother was orchestrating my suffering like a conductor from hell. Even though I was exhausted, I was grateful to get out of bed when I opened my eyes to sunlight on my bedroom walls.

I called my friend Dave at Veterans' Cab to pick me up and 10 minutes later I heard him tap his horn when he pulled up at the curb. Some folks might call me lazy for not taking the Belt Line streetcar to my office as I usually did. But I saw no point in navigating the two long blocks along slippery sidewalks from my apartment to King Street and risk falling on my keister or worse.

Dave jumped out to open the car door as I approached. "How you doing, Sarge? Saw your picture in last night's *Spec*. Jeez, it must've been a terrific shock to find a corpse at your door."

I sighed. At least he hadn't remarked upon my appearance in that photo.

"I didn't even recognize you at first. Thought it was one of those bums the cops throw in the drunk tank."

I shot him my hard look, the one that said "T'ain't funny McGee" and slid onto the front seat. "Let's go, Dave. I'm late for work."

At my office I tried to open the door but it banged against something hard. My body tensed. I was still jumpy from yesterday's ordeal.

"Just a moment." I relaxed at the sound of Phyllis's voice. Then she swung the door open. "Oh, it's you, Max. Good morning."

In her hands was a length of green garland that trailed onto the floor at her feet. "I'm just about finished decorating the office for Christmas. Isabel thought it was a good idea too."

I glanced at Iz as she stood up from her desk, the hint of a grin on her face. She wore a tailored green dress this morning, a Christmassy complement to her striking red hair. "Take a seat on the couch, Max. I just got some coffee from the White Spot."

The large window facing King Street was draped with some of that garland, and a pint-sized artificial Christmas tree squatted on the coffee table. I hung up my coat and hat, then sat on the couch. There was even a string of silver foil letters spelling "Merry Christmas" tacked above the doorway to my office. I sighed.

Phyllis stowed the small step-ladder in the closet and perched on the edge of the couch beside me, her face aglow. "So how do you like it, Max? It's pretty jolly, isn't it?"

"Very jolly. Thanks for brightening up the place." I figured it was part of my job to bolster the staff's morale even though I wasn't yet in the swing of the festive season.

In fact, I hadn't been in that swing since the war years. I'd spent two Christmases in a men's canteen in England: both were melancholic times, brief bursts of forced goodwill in the face of Jerry's bombing raids. Then a Christmas in Normandy while I was attached to a British regiment after that raid on Dieppe. The following year I was back in England with the Canadians, preparing for the Normandy invasion. Then, after nearly losing my leg during the D-Day landing, I spent the next Christmas in a

British hospital where the so-called joy of the blessed season was in short supply.

Since being back in Canada, with those wartime experiences further and further behind me, I was beginning to swim with the tide.

But not the Yuletide, it seemed.

Isabel joined me in my office and pulled up a chair beside my desk. "Looks like you haven't quite recuperated from yesterday, Max. I can't blame you for that."

"I'm feeling a lot better than the guy who got his picture in *The Spec*."

"If you say so."

Then she leaned across the corner of my desk, sliding her right arm around my neck. "I'm here if you want to talk about it."

We remained like that for a long moment, almost nose to nose, and I could barely speak. "You're a peach, Iz."

She kissed the tip of my nose, then picked up her notebook from my desk and resumed her seat.

I forced myself to follow her lead even though I hated to break the mood. "What's on the plate for today?"

"Mr. Neatby called just before you came in." She passed me a message slip with a phone number. "Something about the Humane Society."

We'd met Philip Neatby on a case a few months ago; he was a partner with a long-established Hamilton law firm – a helpful, friendly man. He'd been easy to work with when he'd hired Max Dexter Associates a couple of times since to undertake witness background checks and other trial preparation work.

"Right – Mr. Neatby. I happened to run into him on the street the other day. I was supposed to contact him about a cruelty to animals case but … there's been a lot of water under the bridge since then, hasn't there? I'll call him today."

Isabel sat quietly, observing me like a drill sergeant inspecting a new recruit. "You sure you're feeling well enough to be back at work?"

I stood up, took her by the arm and guided her toward the door. "There's no cause for worry. I'm jim-dandy." I changed the subject before she could examine me further. "What are you working on today?"

Her lips pursed into a frown that told me I wasn't fooling her – that she knew I was a mile away from being jim-dandy. "I have an appointment at the Wentworth Law Office this morning."

"Where Emma Rose works."

"That's right. I've kept in touch with her since we met right here in your office, Max."

I picked up on the teasing tone in her voice; even so, the alluring image of the dazzling Emma, whom I'd known from school days, blossomed in my mind. I also remembered Isabel's discomfort when she'd first met her, thinking there might have been, or might still be, something going on between Emma and me. I leaned toward her, eyebrows raised, "So how *is* Emma?"

"She's just fine. And she'd like me to do some accounts analysis work to support a fraud case she's working on. I'm really interested because it's a relatively new field; what they call 'investigative accounting'."

I nodded as if I understood that. Of course she knew I didn't, so she didn't elaborate.

"And I'm taking you to lunch today." A chirpy tone in her voice now. "I've made a reservation at Fischer's Hotel for 12:30."

"Well, thanks. But what's the occasion?"

She took a half-step forward, jutting her chin out. "We don't need a special occasion. I'd just like to take you to lunch."

I couldn't keep the smile off my face. "You know, your eyes seem to sparkle a brighter shade of green when you zing me with one of your looks."

She moved closer and pinched my arm. "Enough of your blarney. If I'm not back by 12:15, I'll meet you at the hotel."

I was grinning as she swished out of my office.

I picked up the note to return Mr. Neatby's phone call and wondered if he might have another job for us.

"I'll see if he's still in his office," his secretary told me. "He has to be in court shortly so he might have left while I was away from my desk."

I waited a moment, then Mr. Neatby came on the line. "Sorry for the delay, Mr. Dexter. I've got to leave in a few minutes so I wondered if you could drop in to see me this afternoon. About two o'clock?"

I glanced at my agenda – no appointments after lunch. "Two's fine. What's it about exactly – animal cruelty or something?"

"Yes. I do the legal work for the Hamilton branch of the Society for the Protection of Cruelty to Animals. In fact, I'm on their Board of Directors. It's a very active affiliate of the Ontario SPCA and I think we'll need some help with an investigation."

"Sounds intriguing – tell me more."

He paused briefly then cleared his throat. "I'd rather not say on the phone. I'll see you at two."

I plopped the receiver back on its cradle, wondering what would keep him from speaking about animals on the phone.

Later, Phyllis tapped on my office door and poked her head in. "There's a woman on the line who insists on speaking with you, Max. But she won't give me her name. Do you want me to take her number?"

"No, I'll talk to her. Thanks."

I picked up the receiver.

"Hullo." A sultry voice. "This is Diane Black calling."

I drew a blank. "Sorry, you must have the wrong number."

"It's your mother, Max. I have a new name now. As well as a new life."

I rocked back in my chair as if I'd been rammed in the chest. I looked at the receiver in my hand as though I'd never seen a phone before. What do you say to a mother who abandoned you as a child? A woman who had the same regard for you as she might have for a piece of used furniture or an old coat. A woman whose presence here may have contributed to Bernie Fiore's murder and his disposal on my doorstep. Righteous anger raced along my nerve endings as my grip tightened on the receiver.

"Why are you calling me? Why now, after more than 20 years?"

She paused a long beat before answering. "I don't think I can give you an answer that will satisfy you – and certainly not on the telephone. My decision to leave Hamilton had much more to do with your father than it did with you. But I can understand why you're upset."

"I don't think you have the slightest idea why I'm upset. You don't know anything about me. I'm hanging up now."

"Wait, Max," an urgency in her voice. "I need to see you. There's something I have to discuss with you. It's very important. I've made a reservation at Robert's Restaurant for 7:00 this evening. Please don't disappoint me."

She hung up before I could.

I replaced the receiver, questions somersaulting through my mind but no answers in sight. Something important, but she couldn't tell me on the phone. I was madder than hell but in the end I knew I'd probably meet her. Sometimes I was just too damn curious for my own good.

It seemed that an ordinary day was a thing of the past; so far, there hadn't been much business happening in my new business. And I'd received two phone calls, but both callers said they couldn't explain their business on the phone.

And two women had made plans for me: one for lunch, the other for dinner. If this kept up, I wouldn't have to think for myself anymore.

CHAPTER EIGHT

Iz AND I STOOD OUT of the weather in the entranceway of the *Spectator* building. The light snow had changed to an icy mix so I'd called for a cab to take us to lunch. As we waited she angled her head toward the Capitol Theatre, just a couple of doors west.

"They're still showing *Miracle on 34th Street*. There's a little girl in the movie – I think the young actress is Natalie Woods, or some name like that, and she was so sweet. I saw it last week with a couple of my school friends from Loretto Academy days – we keep in touch from time to time."

"Even after all these years?"

She delivered an elbow to my ribs. "Watch your step, Mister. It wasn't that long ago."

I was scanning King Street for our cab, listening to Iz with one ear; the taxi stand across the street at the Royal Connaught Hotel was empty, due to the weather I supposed.

"My friends, Greta and Frankie, both married well," she was saying. "And they keep reminding me that I'm not getting any younger."

"What's that mean, 'they married well'?"

She turned to face me and our eyes locked. "You know, their husbands are rich and they're able to live in comfort."

I let that sink in; it didn't fit *my* profile. "So their husbands aren't daring and adventurous like me?"

She puckered her lips as though she doubted my Errol Flynn attributes.

The wind picked up and I stood closer, sliding my arm around her waist. "Are you jealous of your friends for marrying well?"

"Certainly not, Max. I'm holding out for someone daring and adventurous."

A Veterans' Cab pulled to the curb and the driver jumped out to open the door. I saw it was Dave again. I'd met him last summer and when he'd learned we'd both seen action at Dieppe, he'd more or less adopted me as my regular driver. He fussed over Isabel, saying what a pleasure it was to finally meet her, he'd heard so much about her from Max. Of course, I hadn't told him a damn thing other than her name. "Let's get this show on the road, Dave. We don't want to be late for lunch."

During the short drive to Fischer's Hotel on York Street it seemed he couldn't shut up. We heard all about the "snow storm of the century" in 1944. "Shoulda seen it, Max. It was a week or two before Christmas, just like now. And it snowed so much that downtown traffic was snarled for nearly a week. Isn't that right, Isabel?"

It was a relief when we stopped at the entrance to the hotel. Dave leapt out to hold the door for Isabel, bowing as if she were Princess Elizabeth. And I wondered why some guys were reduced to Jell-O in the presence of a beautiful woman.

Fischer's was a swanky place, all dressed up for the season – the dining room was to the left of a spacious lobby dominated by a floor-to-ceiling Christmas tree which had been sprayed pink and decorated with oversized silver bulbs. I'd never seen a pink tree and it wasn't as bad as I might've thought. A colourful poster near the entrance read: THIS FRIDAY NITE ONLY: *Dance to the rhythmic stylings of CBC Radio Star, Bert Niosi and his Trio.*

Our waiter showed us to a table in a quiet corner of the cozy room, past the long smorgasbord spread where the competing aromas of a wide variety of foods I couldn't even identify added an international flavour. We'd just begun reading our menus when a good-looking gent approached; he wore a snazzy blue double-breasted suit with a red rose in his lapel.

"Wonderful to have you back again, Miss O'Brien. Long time no see."

Isabel smiled at him, then turned to me. "This is Bud Fischer, Max. He's the owner of this hotel."

He extended his hand and I reached for it. "And you must be Max Dexter. Saw your picture in the paper last night. I'll bet it was quite a shock for you, finding that body."

When he'd finished pumping my hand, I agreed that it was a shock and, yes, I'd just about recovered now, and yes again, I was trying to keep a stiff upper lip and carry on. Then he clamped a big mitt on my shoulder and bent closer. "Pleasure to meet you, Sir. You're a brave man indeed."

He turned toward my partner. "Now, would you like to enjoy the smorgasbord or would you prefer me to send a waiter over to take your order?"

During lunch we chit-chatted about everything except that phone call from Diane Black and her summons to dinner. I was reluctant to bring it up and spoil our Christmassy lunch but I finally gave Iz a full report, such as it was.

She set down her coffee cup and leaned in close. "I know it's a difficult decision for you. I understand completely."

"No, I don't think you do. Our backgrounds are miles apart."

"Not as much as you might think, Max. Not in the things which are really important in life. Listen, my mother left me when I was a child, too. Not voluntarily … she died of pneumonia when I was six years old. I think I missed her as much as you must have missed your mother and we both had inadequate fathers. At least you inherited Frank's family who welcomed you and loved you. But I've never felt the closeness of a warm and caring family.

"I grew up with no mother and a father who spent all his time at the office or travelling on business. In his place, there was a long procession of nannies who treated me like the family pet – I was fed and watered and cleaned and taught to know my place. I ran away twice and was returned both times by the police. I finally settled down when it dawned upon me that I'd have to take charge of my own life and plan for my own future. I did well at school and moved away to university as soon as I could."

Iz hadn't told me much about her childhood and I felt guilty for having assumed she'd had a happy life just because she came from money. "But after you got your accounting degree you went to work in your father's company."

"I needed to get some work experience under my belt before I could go out on my own. And I hoped my father had improved with age – but he hadn't. And now I've changed my plans since meeting you, Max. I like the detective business – it's challenging and it feels good to help people solve their problems." She extended her right hand and gripped mine. "And when I have a family of my own, I hope I'll find the love I haven't known since my mother died."

I leaned back in my chair and sighed. I loved this woman. She took my breath away.

"But I still think you should meet your mother, Max. She's the only one you'll ever have. You could at least listen to what she has to say."

She swivelled in her chair and signaled the waiter for more coffee. I watched her busying herself with her napkin, folding and refolding it. Her little speech nudged me to reconsider my own self-centred position: I had to admit that many people had worked their way through difficult situations, some of them much worse than mine. And I now realized that Isabel was one of those people.

I drew in a couple of deep breaths and submerged my second thoughts before I spoke. "I believe I'm falling in love with you, Isabel O'Brien."

Just then the waiter arrived and refilled our cups, giving us time to consider what I'd just blurted out.

Her smile gleamed like sunlight breaking through the clouds on a bleak November afternoon. "Did you just say 'falling in love', Max?"

"I can't believe I said it either."

She reached across the table with both hands and gripped mine. "I want to give you a great big smooch on the lips."

"I don't think Mr. Fischer would approve."

Iz turned quickly as the owner arrived at our table. He picked up the bill that the waiter had left and slipped it into his jacket pocket. "Lunch is on me, folks. I hope you come back again soon. And a Merry Christmas to you both."

I was impressed by his generosity. Then I figured he might have seen it as a form of advertising; leaving us with a good feeling, hoping we'd become regular customers. And who knew? Maybe we would.

In the cab on the way back to the office, Iz clutched my hand and nestled her head on my shoulder. She whispered in my ear, "He said he's falling in love with me."

I whispered back. "And what does she think about that?"

"She thinks the feeling's mutual."

"You'll have to speak up," Dave said. "I can't hear you."

CHAPTER NINE

DAVE DROPPED ISABEL AT THE office, then drove me to James Street South near the corner of Main, where Mr. Neatby's office was located in the eighteen-storey Pigott Building, Hamilton's one and only skyscraper. On my last visit to this building about six months ago, I met with Mr. H.B. Myers – a greedy little businessman who'd met the fate he deserved.

A perky young woman poked her head out from the first in a row of elevators and sent me a bright smile. "Going up?"

She was wearing what looked like a Women's Army Corps uniform, but it was smartly tailored in a vivid shade of blue with a matching wedge cap set at a jaunty angle, and on her hands, a pair of white gloves. As I entered the car I noticed her name was etched on a small brass plate pinned to the pocket over her heart: 'Noretta'. She touched two fingers to her cap in a mock salute, "Which floor, Handsome?"

I gave her a nod and played along. "Just drive. I'll let you know when we're close."

"Oh, my. A wise-guy." She drew the polished brass gate closed, then the elevator doors, and cranked the lever to move us skyward. She half-turned to face me, the feminine fragrance of lavender soap following her motion. "But I don't mind joking with my passengers because it relieves the monotony of this job. Are we close yet?"

"Fifteenth floor."

"Boy, I'm glad you said that. Usually when I say this job's monotonous, most guys think they're comedians and they come out with, 'Yeah, but I bet it has its ups and downs.' If I hear that corny line one more time I think I'll scream." The car came to a smooth stop and she winked at me over her left shoulder. "Here's your floor, Big Boy."

Mr. Neatby's office was on the south side of the building and would have afforded a sweeping view up the mountain if it weren't for the misty fog settling over the escarpment. I was ushered in by a smartly-dressed woman of a certain age who welcomed me with a warm smile. The lawyer rose from his chair: a tall man with a military bearing whose usual good humour seemed muted today.

He extended his hand to greet me and indicated a pair of comfy-looking armchairs near the windows and we settled in. "Before we start, may I offer you some coffee or tea, Mr. Dexter?"

"Not for me, thanks. I just had lunch."

He glanced toward his secretary waiting near the doorway. "That'll be all, thank you, Mrs. Neatby."

Her smile reappeared and she left the office, closing the door behind her. I turned to face him, "Not to be impertinent, but was that your wife?"

"Yes, it was."

"But you called her Mrs. Neatby."

The merest trace of a grin quivered at the corners of his mouth. "We like to observe a certain amount of business decorum here in the office."

I thought about that. Maybe it was just a lawyerly thing but it seemed old-fashioned to me. Then again, maybe he was pulling my leg and the little act I'd just witnessed was a refined example of lawyer humour. You never knew with these legal eagles.

I withdrew my notebook and flipped to a blank page. "So ... the Humane Society."

"Let me give you a little background first. The Hamilton branch of the SPCA was founded in 1887 by a small group of private citizens and the main concern back then was the humane treatment of working animals. It wasn't as common for people to keep animals as pets in those early years, so the Society's efforts were focused on preventing the abuse of horses for deliveries of all kinds, including the Hamilton Street Railway, as well as farm animals that were often overworked or maltreated. With the introduction of trucks and motor cars, of course, we're seeing fewer large animals in the city but many more stray cats and dogs and other pets.

"Early on, our committee was able to convince the City to appoint a part-time constable from the Police Department to enforce the laws against cruelty to animals. In addition, the City provided a small annual grant to hire a part-time inspector to issue fines to offenders; he also inspected animals sold at the Hamilton Market for human consumption to ensure they were free of illness. And that remains the situation today."

I stopped him there. "So the Society's still a volunteer organization?"

"That's right. We have a Board of Directors composed of local people and there are several active committees – educational activities, fund-raising and so forth. Raising awareness among the public remains one of our most important objectives and we've done very well in that regard, if I may say so. For example, our Women's Committee has encouraged teachers and principals to include humane education in the classroom. At the end of 1946 our adult membership was over a thousand and the junior members numbered 14,000."

He leaned back in his chair, eyebrows raised, allowing me time to be impressed by the Society's success. And I was. "I didn't know there are so many members, especially kids. It's a great idea to spark their interest when they're young."

Mr. Neatby accepted my praise with a nod and continued. "But we can't afford to rest on our laurels. We're in desperate need of a proper shelter for abused animals and, of course, the personnel to operate it. Right now, the City Works Department staff picks up stray or abandoned animals and keeps them for a short time at the equipment yards on Elgin Street, just beside the Barton Street Jail."

"Then what happens to them?"

"They're only kept for a day or so. Then they're 'put to sleep'."

I read the frustration in his eyes and we didn't speak for a moment; it seemed as if we'd somehow agreed to observe a moment of silence for the abused, sick and stray animals that had been euthanized.

"I wish you well in your campaign to build a shelter," I said. "But what did you want to see me about today?"

"Well, I mentioned earlier that we rely upon the police to carry out investigations in cases of serious abuse. But they're busy with their regular duties and the assignment of a part-time constable just isn't enough to satisfy the need. So our campaign will also raise funds to hire a full-time manager for the shelter who'll have the authority to investigate and lay charges under the Criminal Code of Canada."

He paused for a moment to take a sip of water from a glass on a small tray beside him and the fussy way he put down the glass, placing it just so on the tray, told me we were finally coming to the point of this meeting. I leaned forward in my chair.

"Recently we've received a complaint about the abuse of dogs on a property on Parkdale Avenue, out by the Municipal Airport. It appears to be a criminal matter and since I provide legal services to the Society's Board, it's been referred to me."

"What kind of criminal matter?"

"The property owner is suspected of staging dog fights. I don't know how much you know about this so-called blood sport, but it's a nasty business, Mr. Dexter."

While he took another sip of water, I asked him, "What kind of dogs are used in these fights?"

He set down his glass. "They're commonly known as 'pit bulls' – a result of crossbreeding bulldogs, mastiffs and terriers over many years so that now they're a heavily muscled breed and they're trained to fight to the death.

"As far as we know, there are only a few breeders and trainers in the Hamilton area but we do hear about these fights from time to time. It's an illegal, underground activity, pitting dog against dog, and the results are truly horrifying. Gamblers are usually in attendance to bet on these fights; drugs and alcohol are common and, according to the police, the entire enterprise is controlled by the Mafia."

"So why don't they raid the fights and arrest the offenders?"

"I wish it were that simple. These fights are usually held late at night in out-of-the-way locations like the one we're talking about, and local residents don't always report them because they fear reprisal from the landowner or even the gangsters. And if the police show up after the event, as they did in this case, there's not much they can do about it. You see, it's not illegal in Ontario to raise and train these fighting dogs."

"Well, that sounds stupid. Why else would someone train the dogs if it weren't to fight them?"

"You're right – it does *not* make sense. That's why the Ontario SPCA and its affiliates have been lobbying the government to change the law."

He paused for a moment or two, giving me some time to think about it. "What would you like me to do?" I finally asked him.

"I believe you're a very good detective, Mr. Dexter, and I appreciated the sensitive way in which you handled the interests of my client, Grace Clark, when her employer was murdered a few months ago. So I hope you'll agree to look into this matter for us – perhaps talk to some of the neighbours out there, maybe even speak with the owner under some pretext. We need some evidence in order to stop these vicious fights."

His dark eyes held mine as he absently tapped the fingers of his right hand on a brown envelope beside his desk blotter. But what could I do if even the cops were stymied because of the inadequate laws? So I waited him out. He looked at me, and I looked at that envelope.

Lawyers are better at this game than I am and I folded first. "I presume I'd be paid my usual daily rate?"

"We'd both be paid the same."

I was afraid of that and I braced myself. "Which is?"

"As a member of the board, my services are *pro bono*."

Shit, just as I'd thought. "Jeez, I don't know if I'd have the time and I'm kind of busy right now –"

He held up his right hand to cut me off and withdrew a red file folder from that brown envelope on his desk and passed it to me. "Before you decide, please take a look at these photographs."

I opened the folder and caught my breath. The pictures showed wounded and bleeding dogs, some with their eyes gouged out, the bloody remains of ears bitten off; others with their throats ripped open and deep oozing scratches on their legs and undersides. Here was another with blood gushing from two big punctures in the back of its head, dying as Bernie Fiore had died before he'd been dumped on my porch. It was all I could do to keep from retching.

I'd faced the horror of mutilated bodies during the war, but this was different – these dogs were maimed and slaughtered during peacetime, at the hands of depraved people for their *entertainment.* Most of the photos were close-ups of the dead and dismembered animals, but the one that hit me the hardest showed the leering faces of sweating gamblers leaning forward across a wooden enclosure, some with money clutched in their fists, screaming at the dogs to rip their opponents apart, to kill them. Those photos were so vivid they almost reeked with the sweet-sour odour of blood and booze and cigar smoke.

I flipped quickly through the rest of the stack and took my time closing my notebook, and replaced it in my suit jacket. Forcing myself to swallow the bile rising in my throat, I pointed to an empty glass on the tray beside Mr. Neatby; he filled it from the pitcher and passed it to me.

I gulped it down and returned the glass. "So this is why they call it a 'blood sport'?"

He nodded as he slid the photos back into their envelope. "It's cruel and contemptible. Now you see why it's urgent that we stop this vicious practice as soon as possible."

My eyes drifted to the window behind him, distracted by the busy snowflakes now changing to rain as the outdoor temperature increased a couple of degrees – in the same way that Mr. Neatby had increased the temperature on my conscience, hoping to change me into an active supporter of animal rights. He was a clever man, discerning that I might become a convert to his cause because it was the right thing to do. Even for no pay.

"Give me a few days. I'll see what I can do but I can't promise you anything."

He rose to his feet and we shook hands. "That's all I ask, Mr. Dexter. The Society appreciates your assistance."

He helped me on with my coat then handed me my fedora.

"By the way," I said. "Thanks for not mentioning that picture in *The Spectator.*"

He squinted at me. "What picture was that?"

"Oh, nothing." I waved my hand. "Forget it."

CHAPTER TEN

WHEN I LEFT THE PIGOTT Building, the sidewalks were wet but not slippery. So I decided to hike back to my office to clear my mind, still reeling in the after-image of those gruesome photographs coming so soon after yesterday's shock.

I joined a small knot of pedestrians gathered near the display windows at Robinson's Department Store where a Salvation Army band was playing "O Little Town of Bethlehem". I stood beside an old duffer tapping his cane on the sidewalk in time to the music. My eye was drawn to the cornet player – a shapely young woman even in her drab blue uniform with the old-fashioned bonnet. The guy on the bass drum and the euphonium player were doing their best to drown her out.

My mind flashed to a vivid image from that Damon Runyon story about another Salvation Army woman, Miss Sarah Brown, who meets the gambler, Sky something-or-other, and tries to persuade him to tread the straight and narrow. It made me wonder how similar that odd pairing was to Isabel and me – probably closer than I cared to think.

I dropped a two-dollar bill in the big collection kettle beside the tambourine player and she gave me a Christmas smile in return.

At the corner of King and James, I glanced up at the huge billboard mounted on the roof of the United Cigar Store building – BUY TB CHRISTMAS SEALS – and I wondered what this time of year would be like for all those folks in the crowded sanitarium up on the mountain. Christmastime in the san. Didn't sound too jolly to me.

Black clouds were rolling in as the wind off the bay picked up and swirled along King Street. An ominous clap of thunder and a sudden crack of lightning sent pedestrians scattering for shelter. I began to limp on the double and almost at once my mind was under siege – I was diving for cover from the German artillery blasting down from the heights over Dieppe's bloodied beach; then an angry pack of fighting dogs was racing behind me – snarling and drooling, their bloody jaws snapping while Bernie Fiore's accusing eyes followed me. I tried to hurry even faster, attempting to leave those images behind me, but they were hot on my heels as if the dogs had my scent.

I straggled into my building and slumped against the wall beside the doors, panting as I caught my breath and drove those terrifying images from my mind. And I wondered if these flash-backs would ever end. Would Isabel consider me damaged goods if she knew how often my mind was overtaken with those wartime memories of violence and death? Shell shock or battle fatigue, they called it. Army doctors had assured me those memories would go away in due course. I'd say that course was overdue.

Outside, the sleety rain was now turning to wet snow and a clutch of pedestrians had followed me in, shaking the melting snow from their coats; they reminded me of house cats who'd been caught outside in a sudden downpour.

Back in my familiar surroundings I felt my black mood begin-ning to lift. When I entered my office, Phyllis relieved me of my coat and hung it up for me. I said, "Thank you, Miss Evans." No harm in introducing a certain business decorum into the office.

Her eyebrows lifted and she sent me a puzzled look. "You're welcome, Mr. Dexter."

I flipped my damp fedora onto the filing cabinet by the door-way. "Isabel back soon?"

She glanced at her wristwatch. "She said about 3:30, depend-ing on how talkative Emma Rose is today."

I reviewed my notes from the meeting with Mr. Neatby, then pushed my chair back from the desk, staring out the window. Here was another situation that might bring some involvement with the city's criminal underworld. Should I really take the risk of tangling with those mobsters again? Especially since Isabel and I were becoming closer. In fact, a lot closer.

To be honest, I wanted both. I was fascinated as well as appalled by the Mob and the bold swagger of its bosses – Rocco Perri, Al Capone, Stefano Maggadino, and Dominic Tedesco – all larger than life figures who scoffed at society's rules and regulations. I was strangely fascinated by them, but it annoyed the hell out of me that these guys could so frequently get away with murder and a laundry list of other crimes. I wanted to do my part, however small, in bringing the bastards to justice.

But I also wanted the love of a woman who shared my convictions and was willing to raise a family with me. Was it possible to have both? That was the 64-dollar question.

When Isabel returned from her meeting, she breezed into my office and sat beside me at the long table against the wall. "Tell me about your mysterious meeting with Mr. Neatby. You said he didn't want to speak about it on the phone."

"Because he had some pictures to show me. He wanted to soften me up before he made his proposition."

She raised her right eyebrow. "An undercover job?"

"Not exactly. Mr. Neatby's the lawyer for the Hamilton SPCA and he wants me to look into a suspected case of staging dog fights, an offence under the Criminal Code. He showed me some photographs of dead and wounded dogs – the losers in those fights. A horrible sight, Iz."

She winced. "But what does he want you to do?"

"Snoop around, mainly. There's a guy in the east end of the city who might be arranging these fights and we'd need some evidence to bring a charge against him." I hesitated a moment before I continued. "Tedesco and his troops might be involved too. They're suspected of organizing the betting, the booze and the drugs."

Her eyes were downcast and she appeared to be inspecting the pale pink polish on her nails while I spoke. When she looked up there was a spark in her eyes and I couldn't tell if it signified her fear that I may be involving us with Tedesco again or her revulsion at the practice of fighting dogs. Maybe both.

"It sounds positively medieval, Max. Are you sure you want to get mixed up in this?"

"No, I'm not sure. But I told Mr. Neatby I'd look into it and let him know. However, the pay's not great."

"Don't tell me. *Pro bono*?"

"A small investment of time to cement our relationship with Mr. Neatby and to ensure his future business."

"Oh, Brother." She was shaking those red curls. "You're such an old softie, Max."

CHAPTER ELEVEN

I WAS PACING THE SMALL area between the window and my desk, having a terrible time keeping my mind on business this afternoon. Every few minutes I'd find myself daydreaming, staring out the window or doodling in the margin of my note pad. My thoughts kept returning to Isabel, snuggled up beside me in Dave's cab after lunch. And every time I heard her speak in the outer office my heart did a little flutter. Jeez Louise, I was behaving like a lovesick teenager.

Then I thought about dinner with my mother and wondered again if it was a bonehead play to meet with her. Iz and I had discussed it once more when she'd gotten back from her meeting and I was relieved when she'd offered to go with me this evening. I knew I could rely upon her to keep me from making a fool of myself, if it came to that.

I pushed my notes aside with relief when Frank Russo phoned.

"How's tricks, Max? No more visitors last night?"

"Didn't hear anyone. But thanks for sending that watchdog."

He paused and it made me wonder if he had some news. "What's happening, Frank?"

"Bernie Fiore's funeral is tomorrow and I wondered if you might want to ride out to the cemetery with me."

"Jeez, I don't know about *that*. And why are you going? You weren't a friend of Bernie's."

"No, I wasn't. But we're making it a practice now to keep an eye on the people who attend these Mob funerals. We have a photographer with one of those long-view lenses so he can stay out of sight while he gets close-up photos of some of these characters."

"Holy hell, Frank. You already know who the local Mob guys are. And you won't get any big-time gangsters from out of town for Bernie's funeral, he was too small a fish."

"You're only half right, smart-ass. They wouldn't come if it were just for him. But your mother's in town and she's a VIP in Mob circles. So we'd like to know who might attend in order to meet with her or Tedesco. We might even have a few of the big Mob bosses show up for a get-together under the guise of attending Bernie's funeral."

"What makes you think my mother's such a bigwig?"

"The Chief got a call from the RCMP last week, passing on information received from the FBI – they've been keeping an eye on the Florida Mob where your mother's well connected. When they learned she was coming to Hamilton they asked us to keep tabs on her while she's here."

"Well, shit, Frank. Thanks for finally letting me know."

"Keep your shirt on; I just found out about it this morning – the brass here keeps that kind of info hush-hush and there was no reason for me to be in the know. But now, with Bernie's death and his brother in jail for the murder of that Planning Committee guy, my boss told me about it because I've been assigned Bernie's case as well as Nick's."

"But my mother wouldn't have knowledge of either one of them, would she? They're just a couple of soldiers."

"That's true. The boss just wanted to give me the full picture."

I thought about what he'd told me; if the Hamilton coppers, not to mention the FBI, were "interested" in my mother then maybe Frank was being pressured to squeeze me for any tidbit I might know about her. But he knew I'd had no contact with her since she left town all those years ago. He also knew that I'd kick up a helluva fuss if he tried to recruit me as a police spy.

"Are you under the gun, Frank? Does your boss want you to enlist me as an unofficial pair of eyes, watching and reporting on my mother?"

I listened to him chuckle in my ear. "Can't pull a fast one on you, eh, Maxie? Yeah, that's exactly what he asked me to do. I told him you didn't know a damn thing about her – that we'd grown up together as brothers and I'd know if you'd been in contact with her."

"So now you've got, what, a couple of guys following her around?"

"Just a loose surveillance, seeing who she meets, that type of thing."

I thought about our plans to meet my mother for dinner tonight. I didn't want to place Isabel in the centre of a police investigation. Or myself, for that matter. And I hesitated about telling Frank about meeting her. But, hell, he'd find out anyway and then he'd be pissed that I hadn't tipped him off. And I'd never place our lifelong friendship in jeopardy.

"What time's the funeral?"

"Mass is at 0900 at All Souls, then burial in Holy Sepulchre, probably about 1100 or so. But if you're really keen you can say the rosary this evening at Dermody's Funeral Home just beside St. Pat's Church there. 1930."

"Sorry, but I can't make it for the rosary. Isabel and I are meeting my mother for dinner tonight."

I heard him catch his breath before he nearly shattered my eardrum, "WHAT?"

"You heard me, Frank. Robert's Restaurant. 1900."

He didn't respond right away and I listened to his heavy breathing on the line, imagining his face turning purple and steam jetting from his ears. But his voice was subdued, even chilly. "You sure that's a good idea?"

"No, I'm not at all sure. In fact, it's probably a stupid idea. But we're going to do it anyway. I can't explain it to you, Frank, it's just something I have to do – even if she's the FBI's Public Enemy Number One."

I heard him clear his throat, probably deciding between coming over to my office to wring my neck or simply firing me as his kid brother. But he managed to keep his voice calm. "Do you want to go to the funeral or not?"

"Yes, I do." If my mother was as well connected with the Mob as the police believed, then I'd like to see with my own eyes how she might conduct herself with all those gangsters who might be attending the funeral because of her presence.

"Okay, then. I'll pick you up at your apartment in the morning – about 1000 and we'll go straight out to the cemetery. And Maxie?"

"Yeah?"

"Be careful tonight. You don't know what kind of woman your mother is – or anything about her. Just – don't do anything stupid."

I hung up the phone and sank back in my chair. Six months ago, I wouldn't have hesitated to mix it up with Tedesco's gang as long as Frank was by my side. But things were different now – I hoped for a life with Isabel and a family of our own. And poking your nose into the Mob's business was an easy way to get it blown off. On the other hand, seeing my mother again was something I'd wondered about most of my life. I had my chance now, and I wasn't going to give it up.

I opened my office door and asked Iz to step in.

She sat by my desk, questions in her eyes. "You look worried, Max. Tell me."

She leaned forward on the edge of her chair as I related Frank's conversation. "It's up to you," I said when I'd finished. "You can back off if you're worried about meeting her. Maybe it was selfish of me to accept your offer to come with me."

"Let's not jump the gun, Max. Give me a moment to think about this."

I watched her in profile as she sat back and gazed out my office window. She could have jumped at my suggestion to back off but she hadn't. No, she was weighing the pros and cons in her cool and rational manner. I waited, observing her as she controlled her breathing, then smoothed the wrinkles from her skirt before drawing back a wayward red curl from her forehead with a long finger. A smart and beautiful woman. I still couldn't believe my luck.

She inhaled a deep breath, let it out slowly, then turned to face me. "If the police are watching your mother it should be safe for us to meet her. But there's a bigger concern: if she's as important in the crime world as the police think she is ... maybe we shouldn't have anything to do with her at all."

"That's the big question, isn't it? I've often wondered if I'd ever see her again. And you know me, Iz, I'm a curious guy – so I'm anxious to know why she wants to meet me now."

Her eyes were fixed on mine while I spoke. Then she gulped, swallowing whatever misgivings she might've had, and stood up, extending her hand. "We're in this together, Max." And we shook on it.

Later, I heard desk drawers and filing cabinets opening and closing in the outer office and I checked my old Bulova. Quitting time.

Isabel stood at the entrance to my office, wearing her red winter coat with a small black velvet hat.

"Spiffy outfit," I waggled my eyebrows. "Going out tonight?"

"Yes, I am." Her lips twitched as she strained to keep a straight face. "My beau is taking me to dinner. To meet his mother."

"Your beau?"

"Well, I guess you could call him that. He's given me every indication that his intentions are sincere."

"Sounds like a smart fellow." I moved closer, lowering my voice as I touched her arm. "Not to mention daring and adventurous."

"He'll have to save that for later, Max. We've got just enough time for me to drop you at your apartment, go home to change my dress and pick you up at 6:45." She reached forward to straighten my tie then brushed at something on my lapel with the back of her hand. "But what if your mother doesn't want me there?"

"Then we'll leave and that'll be the end of that."

CHAPTER TWELVE

THE SLEET AND RAIN FROM this afternoon had given way to clear skies and a dip in the temperature when Iz picked me up at my apartment. I slid across the front seat of her 1947 Studebaker coupé and pecked her on the cheek. "How's my apple dumpling?"

Her lips were pursed but there was a glint in her eyes as she shook her head. "You're something special, Max."

Then she drove straight down King Street to Sanford Avenue where Robert's Restaurant was kitty-corner from the Hamilton Street Railway's car-barns.

She found an empty parking space beside the restaurant and I took her arm as we navigated the shadowy lot. We were walking alongside the building toward the entrance when two burly figures darted from the shadows and grabbed us, pinning us both against the wall.

The taller thug twisted my right arm up behind me, smacking the side of my face against the rough bricks, knocking my hat to the ground. The other guy had his left hand clamped over Isabel's mouth after dragging her over beside me. She faced in my direction, her right cheek pressed hard against the building. And she had fire in her eyes.

"If it's money you're after," I said, "you've come to the wrong bank."

"We ain't looking for dough, wiseacre. Relax – it's just a friendly pat-down."

My guy did thorough work – he ran his hands up and down my arms and legs, checked my waist for a gun stuck in my pants, then my coat pockets.

The left side of my face was grinding against the building as I watched the other guy checking Isabel's coat, then her purse.

"She's clean," he told his partner.

A wave of relief rolled over me when my face came away from the wall. Then the guy spun me around. He snatched up my hat from the ground, brushed it off with his coat sleeve and plunked it on my head. "Pardon the delay," he said. "Enjoy your evening."

Isabel shivered in my arms as we watched them slink away and slip into a long black Fleetwood parked at the rear of the lot.

"Let's get out of here," I said. "I had mixed feelings about this meeting. Now I'm convinced it's a bum idea."

Wearing her high heels, she was the same height as me and we huddled there at the side of the building, eye to eye without speaking for a moment. "Not a chance, Max. We've come this far and undergone this humiliation. Now we're going to follow through and meet your mother."

I took a step back, my hands on her shoulders, as our eyes locked. "I hadn't realized just how determined you can be. My apple dumpling has a thicker skin than I thought."

We entered the restaurant lobby from King Street; I glanced to my right where a wide curving stairway wound its way to the second floor. A vibrant banner suspended at the top of the stairs read: *Welcome to the Rainbow Room. One of Ontario's Smartest Ballrooms.*

The coat check was on the main level and a flirty young woman batted her eyes at me as she took our coats and my fedora. But first I had to do a better job of brushing it off than the guy in the parking lot had managed. She passed me the check stubs and a smile. "Here you go, Big Fella. Have fun tonight."

Isabel rolled her eyes at me then excused herself and entered the ladies' restroom to "repair her makeup after that bit of business outside".

I stepped into the gents' and looked myself over in the mirror. I straightened my tie, removed some lint from my jacket and combed my hair with my hands. But my shaggy mop refused to lie flat. I needed a haircut but I never seemed to make time for it. I hated to admit it, but I saw a strong resemblance to that guy in the *Spec* photo. So I made an early New Year's resolution to take better care of my appearance.

Back in the lobby, I stuck my hands in my pockets and looked around as I waited for Iz. There was an air of relaxed anticipation here as chatty couples mounted the staircase to the Rainbow Room while others strolled toward the dining room on this level. I noticed a poster on the wall near the coat check – smiling people wearing party hats and blowing horns, confetti in the air. The copy read:

Reserve now for Gala New Year's Eve in the new Rainbow Room
Dancing to Chris Lovett's Orchestra.
Party Favours and Midnight Buffet.
Only $6 per couple.

When Isabel joined me, we entered the Marine Room where a dapper gent in a tux with a leather-bound menu under his arm was making his way toward us. At that moment, I heard the mellow tone of a tenor saxophone and turned toward a small bandstand nearby where a placard on an easel announced: *The Gord Brown Trio.* They'd just eased into a bluesy version of "White Christmas" and it was a relief not to hear those lyrics for the umpteenth time.

The maître d' welcomed us and I gave him my name. He led us toward a quiet corner table where a stylish woman in a form-fitting black dress rose to greet us. Her long ebony hair curled about her shoulders – a dark version of that slinky *femme fatale*, Veronica Lake.

I felt my heart pounding in my chest as we reached the table and I stopped in my tracks and stared, searching her face – those deep, dark eyes – observing her posture and looking in vain for the slightest resemblance to the woman I'd known as my mother. I saw no similarity to the features that looked back at me when I shaved every morning. Was there some mistake here? Maybe we'd been brought to the wrong table.

Maybe we should leave right now.

I was speechless as this sleek woman moved forward and placed her left arm around my shoulder, then planted a cold kiss on my cheek.

She leaned back to give me the once-over; I believe I saw a look of satisfaction on her handsome, unlined face. "Not bad," she said, almost to herself. "Not bad, at all."

I could have said the same about her but I held my tongue. She was only 19 when she gave birth to me so that would make her about 50 today. But she looked a good 10 years younger – I could hardly believe my eyes. In addition, she had that certain movie-star allure about her. But I'd be damned if I'd tell her any of that.

She turned toward my partner, appraising Iz with a cool smile. "So this is Isabel O'Brien. I've heard so much about you." Her eyes flicked up. "And I'm jealous of your ravishing, red hair."

The two women locked eyes, their facial expressions calm, almost casual. But beneath that façade I saw a pair of Amazon gladiators, sizing each other up, preparing for battle. While they were shaking hands I wondered what my mother had heard about Isabel. And who the hell had told her?

"I've been curious about meeting Max's mother," Iz said. "But what should we call you?"

"I changed my name to Diane Black after I left Hamilton years ago. For … practical reasons. So please, call me Diane. Both of you. Now sit down, won't you? Max and I have some catching up to do."

Boy, was that was an understatement.

After we took our seats I continued to fight with myself, attempting to keep my anger in check. What could I say to my mother, this glamorous stranger now throwing me off kilter? I could ask her why she left me; if she ever thought about her son; if she had other children – my half-brothers or sisters.

But I didn't.

Instead, I fixed her with my hard look and let my anger speak. "We didn't appreciate your welcoming party in the parking lot. Having us frisked by a couple of gangsters was" – I fumbled for the right words – "rude and unnecessary."

Her gaze didn't waver as she heard me out. "I agree. I didn't know that would happen and I apologize. You know, some men never do grow up. They can't stop playing cops and robbers; it becomes a habit."

I thought about Tedesco and his gang of thugs and I believed she was right on that score. They really were playing cops and robbers, but with live ammunition and deadly consequences.

After we'd settled at the table, the waiter arrived and we ordered the featured prime rib and a bottle of red wine. Then Isabel turned to Diane Black. "Do you mind if I ask why you've come back to Hamilton?"

"Not at all. Of course, you understand I can't go into detail, but I'm a financial management specialist. Let's just say I'm in town to advise some of my associates on a few procedural problems they're experiencing."

Sounded like gobbledygook to me, but this was Isabel's field so I kept my lip buttoned and sent her an encouraging look.

"Financial management," Iz said. "Are you an accountant?"

"Indeed I am." She seemed pleased with my partner's interest and flattered enough to continue. "When I moved to the States I worked with a group that wasn't ..." she waggled her right hand back and forth in a see-saw motion, "developing as well as it might. And I realized I wasn't properly equipped to improve the situation. So I returned to school and earned my Certified Public Accountant's degree."

I watched Isabel's right eyebrow lift. "Well, we have something in common after all. Besides Max."

"I'm well aware of that."

Those gladiators I'd sensed earlier were beginning to move around the arena now.

"Have you heard of Bessie Starkman?"

Iz shook her head.

"Well, Bessie was Rocco Perri's common-law wife. She was the financial brains of Rocco's territory during the 1920s. A very smart woman – she negotiated with Rocco's biggest customers in the U.S. for liquor sales during Prohibition. And certain other transactions as well. I met her a number of times before I moved away."

She paused a moment; a faraway look in her dark eyes. "I guess you could call her a role model of sorts in my later life. She did the type of work I'm doing now; however, my focus is on channeling our resources into developing the real estate market along the Atlantic coast. We're slowly abandoning the old ways of doing business in favour of equity participation in mainstream North American markets."

I gaped at this woman whom I didn't recognize, surprised that she referred to Bessie Starkman with such admiration and thereby admitting that she, too, had devoted herself to a life of crime. I glanced at Isabel who had covered her mouth with her napkin, her eyes wide.

Two waiters arrived at our table; one poured the wine and the other prepared a Caesar salad on a small cart alongside the table and served us.

I ate my salad without tasting it, stealing glimpses of Diane Black from the corner of my eye without drawing her attention. My mind still awhirl with her frank admission that she was an important criminal figure in the U.S. – managing the money for the Florida Mob and, no doubt, other activities I could only guess at. And I began to question again if she really was my mother – this elegant, clever woman who looked nothing at all like that feisty and angry younger version I remembered from my child-hood, the one who hated living with my father and didn't show any interest at all in me. I was having a helluva time trying to reconcile this new image with my jumbled memories.

She set her fork down and turned her attention to me. On her face was that expression, long-buried in the bottom drawer of my subconscious – her upper lip curling slightly at the right corner of her mouth – and it struck me like a shock wave. In that brief moment I was back in the dingy apartment on Hughson Street and she was dismissing my complaint about no supper as she dressed to go out for another evening of dining and dancing and whatever else she did.

And now she was waving her hand in front of my face. "Max, did you hear me? I said that was quite a picture of you in *The Hamilton Spectator*."

While my mind was shifting back to the present, Isabel answered on my behalf. "He prefers not to talk about that."

Diane Black darted a sharp look her way, then turned back to me and changed the subject. "So you're a private detective. Is it interesting work? Do you like it?"

"Yes to both questions. But I'm more and more suspicious of the people I meet these days." I paused, letting that sink in.

"There's often such a chasm between what they say and what they do."

Her eyes held firmly on mine. If she'd taken my remark personally, she didn't show it. "You know, I find the same thing in my line of work."

She turned to Isabel. "How about you, my dear. What's your interest in this detective business?"

Iz didn't respond until the waiter had removed our salad plates. "I'm quite interested in the field of investigative accounting."

Diane Black leaned toward her and spoke with a schoolmarm edge in her voice. "In the U.S. some C.P.A.s refer to this area as 'forensic accounting', meaning it's suitable for use in a court of law."

"Yes, I've been reading up on that. I learned that it's proving to be useful in criminal cases where witnesses are intimidated from testifying. Or they simply disappear. Did you know, for example, that with the help of forensic accountants who specialized in tax fraud, Al Capone was finally prosecuted and sent to jail in 1931 – not for his criminal activities, but for income tax evasion?"

My ears sizzled when I heard Iz mention Al Capone. I had no idea she even knew the gangster's name much less the details of his conviction. And I wondered if she might be sending a not-so-subtle message to this sleek stranger sitting between us.

Diane Black looked closely at Isabel but she didn't respond. When the waiters served us the main course our conversation slowed down to strained exchanges about the weather in Florida compared to Hamilton and other small talk while we ate.

After the coffee was served, my mother turned to me and placed her hand on my arm. "I want you to do something for me."

I couldn't think of a single damn thing I'd want to do for her and my long-simmering anger came to the boil again. I lifted her hand from my arm and pushed it away. Then I leaned toward her, my voice a snake's hiss. "You've got a helluva nerve, Lady. Barging back into my life after an absence of 25 years. In all that time you didn't even send me so much as a goddamn postcard. And now you want *me* to do something for *you*?"

My outburst drew the attention of diners at nearby tables. Iz was staring at me. But Diane Black remained as unperturbed as if I'd complimented her on her appearance.

She continued in a hushed tone, ignoring my outburst. "I'm in a very risky business. It's rooted in a culture of violence and I don't believe that will change for a long time. We have a situation here in Hamilton that requires the retirement of Mr. Tedesco. Certain *excesses* have occurred which have focused unwanted attention on our various enterprises. These things happen from time to time and it's necessary to take corrective action."

She spoke in a flat, dispassionate tone; a business analyst's description of a minor problem that required an adjustment. When she said "excesses", the image of the dead and mutilated body of that City Councillor flashed through my mind. And, of course, Bernie Fiore's punctured and bloodied body dumped on my doorstep. "Excesses" indeed. It was like calling Vesuvius a bonfire.

And now, "corrective action" was on the horizon.

"As you may know," she said, "Mr. Magaddino in Buffalo now controls this territory and arrangements for Mr. Tedesco's successor are underway."

My eyes flicked to Iz; she was staring at my mother, her brow furrowed, her lips pursed and, barely noticeable, her right forefinger tapped lightly on the table.

I was well aware of Stefano Magaddino because I'd worked in the organized crime unit in the RCMP's Toronto office before the war. Magaddino – known as "The Undertaker" – was the long-time Mafia Don who controlled the upper New York State area from his headquarters in Niagara Falls, and later in Buffalo. But it was news to me that he'd taken over the operation in Ontario as well.

I could feel sweat forming in my armpits. Could this really be happening? I was staring at my birth mother, a woman I didn't know and didn't want to know. She was describing a gang war about to erupt: one in which she was squarely in the middle.

"Why are you telling us this?" I said. "You know damn well we'll have to go to the police."

She held my arm again, this time in a tighter squeeze. "Listen carefully, both of you. Tedesco won't relinquish his power easily. He's the type of man who'll try to take down as many of his enemies with him as he can. And he still holds a grudge against you two for interfering in his business; especially you, Max, for shooting his driver a few months ago. He told me about it, before he knew that I was your mother."

I opened my mouth to speak but nothing came out.

She continued to grip my arm, her voice just above a whisper and I caught the frantic look in Isabel's eyes as she leaned in toward us. "I can help you with Tedesco, but I'll need something in exchange."

We waited for her tit for tat as she turned her full attention to me.

"I want you to have a word with your police friend, Russo, because he's in charge of the Fiore investigations."

I could feel my nerve endings tingling and I wondered what else she could know about Frank.

"We need 24 hours to complete our arrangements here and it would complicate matters if the police were to interfere. Now, I understand that Sergeant Russo and his wife have one-year-old twin boys and she's expecting another child. Also, he's got a hefty mortgage which he's just able to cover on his salary. So a family man with his obligations ..." she paused and shrugged her shoulders as though that movement had delivered her message.

When I continued to stare without comment, she said, "He might appreciate a little help with his finances."

Her gaze was steady, watching me for some reaction but I continued to give her nothing in return. She took a sip of her coffee before continuing. "I'm also informed that he has a certain amount of influence with the police brass. So we're prepared to offer Russo a generous Christmas bonus in exchange for delaying his investigation for a couple of days."

Her black eyes gripped mine as she watched me squirm, her audacious proposition worming its way into my brain.

"But if the police are determined to interfere in family business, then responsibility for any civilian casualties will be on their heads."

I slumped back in my chair, not believing my ears. Damn it to hell, she'd just offered to bribe my best friend and now she wants to enlist me as her Judas messenger boy. "What are you talking about? What kind of Christmas bonus? And what kind of casualties?"

A tiny smile tickled the corners of her lips and she might have figured she'd gotten me on board now, or at least thinking about it. "$5,000," she said in a back-alley whisper then she eased back in her chair, watching me stew.

I was struggling to keep calm, aghast that she would attempt to bribe the police. And almost worse, try to use me as her go-between. If she knew anything about me at all, she'd know that I'd never go along with such a scheme. Likewise with Frank – he was more honest than Abe Lincoln. It was true that he could use the money – five grand was about two years' pay for him. But I'd bet my life that he'd tell her to stuff her offer in her ear. Or some-place more awkward.

"Mrs. Black," I snapped out my words, unable to hold back the venom in my voice. "I was raised by the Russo family when my mother abandoned me." I had the odd feeling that I'd just mounted a soap-box in Gore Park but I couldn't stop myself. "Frank Russo is my best friend and I know I speak for him when I tell you – NO. We refuse to be bribed by criminals like you and your henchmen who threaten, rob and even kill those of us who respect the laws of society."

She hadn't budged while I spoke; not a glimmer of reaction appeared on her Hollywood features and I had to marvel at her self-control. And now she seemed to be moving in slow motion as she picked up her purse from beside her chair. "As stubborn as your father," she said in a near-whisper, as though she were talk-ing to herself. "And just as self-righteous."

Then she withdrew a folded piece of paper from her purse and slid it toward me. "My phone number." As I reached for it, she clamped my wrist in her right hand. "If you don't change your mind I may not be able to protect you. Is your precious law worth your life? Think it over. The clock is ticking."

CHAPTER THIRTEEN

IT WAS MUCH COLDER WHEN Isabel and I left the restaurant and we hurried along in silence to the parking lot. No thugs lurked in the shadows and the Caddy had departed. I wondered if the cops who were assigned to "loose surveillance" of Diane Black had even noticed our being frisked.

Driving west on King Street, Iz said, "There's more to your mother than meets the eye."

"That's for damn sure."

"She referred to that woman, Bessie Starkman, as a role model. Do you know about her, Max?"

"I do. She was also known as Bessie Perri but she and Rocco were never married. She was such a powerful force in his outfit that with her help he was able to control the rackets in most of Ontario – booze, gambling, drugs, all that stuff. Then, in 1930, she was murdered; gunned down in the driveway of their big home on Bay Street South, not twenty minutes from here. Some say she'd become too powerful, that Rocco and some of his gang members came to resent her. Others claim that Rocco's business partners were actually gunning for him but murdered Bessie by mistake."

Iz pulled over and stopped at the curb, across the street from St. Patrick's Church, and I noticed that, though she was gripping the steering wheel hard, her hands still trembled. She kept the engine running. "What a grisly story, Max. But surely your mother doesn't have anything to do with that rough stuff, does she? Murder and all those things you said in the speech you gave back there?"

I gave her a sidelong glance, but I guess it was a speech. "Yes, I believe she does. After my father was killed, she was involved with one of Perri's men and they fled the country together, apparently one step ahead of the cops. Frank heard through his police contacts that they'd settled in Florida where she became a member of the Mob. Later, the man she left with was shot to death during a bank robbery. And now, well, you heard what she said."

A light snow shower had begun, the tiny flakes melting on contact with the warm windshield, changing from one state to another – as Diane Black had apparently done.

Isabel shifted in her seat to face me. "This is so bizarre, Max. I'm having trouble believing it. At dinner she spoke about financial matters and real estate investments. At first, it didn't occur to me that she might be directly involved in those ... other things as well." She pressed her lips together and shivered. "But after she talked about paying off Frank to delay his investigation, well, it's obvious that Diane Black is just like those other criminals I've only read about or seen in the movies."

"You're right."

"And she might meet the same fate as Bessie Starkman."

"She might."

We remained silent, our thoughts overtaken by Diane Black's ominous presence in our lives. By her offer to bribe Frank. By her warning that she couldn't protect us from Tedesco if we didn't cooperate with her.

"You never speak about your childhood, Max. You must have some happier memories about your family."

I hated to even think about that wretched time, but Isabel had every right to know. "I really don't remember a lot – I was just a kid when she left. And the memories I do have are a confusing jumble of screaming arguments, doors banging and parents cursing at each other. When my father was drunk, which was often, there'd be slapping and punching too. I would hide under the bed in my room or run upstairs to Frank's apartment to get away from them. His parents would insist that I sleep at their place until the latest storm blew over."

Her lower lip trembled and her eyes became misty.

I touched her cheek with my fingertips.

"That's so sad, Max. I hadn't realized."

"It happens more often than you'd think. But most families don't talk about it. They're embarrassed or ashamed – especially the kids." I didn't speak for a moment as I faced up to it. "Like me."

She leaned across the seat and smothered me in a hug that left my nerve endings tingling.

Then she whispered in my ear, "Let's go home, Max."

CHAPTER FOURTEEN

FRANK PICKED ME UP AT my apartment in the morning in an unmarked car and we drove out York Street toward Holy Sepulchre Cemetery where Bernie Fiore would be interred. Billowy clouds gathered in the western sky; the CKOC weather guy said flurries were likely.

When I glanced across the front seat at Frank I noticed a tiny blood-stained corner of toilet paper stuck to his chin where he'd cut himself shaving. The heater fan was working overtime so I had to raise my voice, "Sleep in this morning, Frank?"

"No. Why?"

"Your chin – check the mirror."

He examined his mug in the rear-view. "Shit." Then he licked a finger and removed it. "Snoopy bugger," he said. "But, thanks."

Now he looked properly funereal in his dark suit and black tie; his overcoat and hat were flung across the back seat.

"You go to the Mass at All Souls?" I said.

He shook his head. "And I didn't say the rosary at the funeral home either."

As we crossed the High Level Bridge I gazed out across Hamilton Harbour toward the canal and Lake Ontario beyond; the bay, dark as India ink, hadn't begun to freeze over yet, and wavelets lapped at the shoreline. Frank turned right off Plains Road, then left onto the cemetery grounds. Through the leaf-less trees you could see Hamilton's north end across the bay, the steel companies' stacks belching smoke and flames. Maybe not a good omen for Bernie Fiore's eternal destination, if you believed in that kind of thing.

Frank slowed the car, then glided to a stop beside an area of large headstones and mausoleums, far enough away from

Dermody's hearse that we wouldn't be easily noticed by the 25 or 30 people gathered at the open gravesite. He pointed to the glove box. "Binoculars. I brought two pair."

From this distance, we had a clear view of the small gathering. A short priest wearing a purple stole over his winter coat and a black biretta on his head was reading prayers from a missal. An older couple dressed in black huddled beside him, probably Bernie's parents. You could count the number of women on one hand, black veils covering their faces; the men were expressionless, most of them shuffling their feet, looking anxious to leave.

"Two cars behind the hearse," Frank said, lowering his binoculars. "That's Tedesco in the back seat. And is that your mother beside him?"

I focused on a long black Buick Roadmaster. The woman in back wore a black pillbox hat, a dark veil extending over her eyes. "I think so, but it's hard to tell because of that veil."

"We'll know for sure when we see the close-up photos."

We were startled by someone tapping on the driver's window. I recognized Wayne Morgan, one of the cops in Frank's squad; he was hunched down at the window, a black toque pulled down over his ears; his red nose began to drip and he wiped it on his coat-sleeve. Frank opened the window a few inches. "What's up, Morgan?"

"Jeez, I'm freezin' my ass off out here. Photographer says he's finished and wants to leave now."

"To hell with that. Tell him he's not done until we get a shot of every one of these buggers."

"Yeah, well, he says it ain't easy. Couple of these big limos have those dark windows in back."

Frank shook his head. "When the prayers are finished and the casket's been lowered, they'll all be out of their cars to file past and sprinkle some earth on it. Just make sure he gets those pictures or I'll have his balls for bookends."

Morgan grinned at him. "I'd like to see that." He looked over at me. "Hey, there, Max. How goes it?"

"Fine ..." I was about to ask after his glamourous wife but he'd already slipped away. Frank wound up his window and reached for his binoculars.

A sombre line of men had formed at the graveside, moving slowly forward to scatter a token amount of earth on Bernie's casket. The women stayed back; most were fingering their rosary beads, their lips moving.

Another wasted life, I thought; Bernie had probably believed a job in the Mob would be a stroll on Easy Street. And a lot more exciting than sweating it out on the assembly line at National Steel Car or some other big factory, then punching out at the end of his shift, tired and bored like most of the working stiffs in the straight world.

I lowered my binoculars and turned to Frank. "Too damn bad Nick couldn't attend the funeral. He was always so protective of his kid brother."

He shook his head. "Too damn bad they both joined the Mob. Like they say: 'You play with the bull, you get the horns'."

I scanned the line of mourners again, searching for Diane Black. "There's my mother near the hearse, Frank, huddled with a couple of guys I've never seen before. But I don't see Tedesco. Maybe he stayed in his car."

Frank took his time to look them over. "Well, she hasn't changed very much; she's still a looker," and he continued to watch. "Huh, that's interesting," he lowered his glasses and turned toward me. "One of the guys with her is Vincenzo Belcastro, the head of the Mob in Niagara Falls. The Mounties say he's got a finger in the pie on both sides of the border."

Then he continued to keep an eye the trio. "The other guy is facing away from me … c'mon, turn my way, you bugger. There … well, I'll be damned."

I focused my binoculars on the guy who now faced in this direction. He was a much slimmer version of that movie gangster, Edward G. Robinson, but with the same sneery expression.

"That's Freddy Randaccio from Buffalo," Frank said. "He's one of Magaddino's chief lieutenants – and according to the FBI he's been made responsible for all Mob operations in Ontario, including Hamilton. He usually keeps a low profile so something big must be happening to require the personal attention of 'Freddy the Wolf'."

I dropped the binoculars on my lap and leaned back in my seat, wondering how to tell Frank about Diane Black's startling revelation that Tedesco was about to "retire" and that a replacement was waiting in the wings. That might explain why this "Wolf" guy was on hand – to witness the passage of power from one local Mob boss to another.

"Ask me about our dinner with my mother last night."

He gave me a sharp look. "Yeah, I was waiting for *you* to tell *me* about it – in your own sweet time. What did she have to say for herself?"

I mulled over several variations of the truth before answering. "She talked about Tedesco – said that he was out of control and that his retirement was imminent."

"Imminent?"

"Yeah, it means soon."

"I know what the hell it means, you dope. How imminent? Did she say?"

"No, but maybe that's why this so-called Wolf character is standing right there talking to her, not a hundred yards away from us."

Then, another rap on the window – much sharper this time, someone using his car keys as a door knocker. Frank wound his window part way down. A young guy was bending over to poke his nose in.

Frank growled at him, "What the hell do *you* want, Johnny?"

"It's disrespectful of you cops to attend our funerals. This is family, nothing to do with business. You should know that, Russo."

Frank shifted in his seat and leaned closer to him, his words coming out coated with ice. "Thanks for the advice, kid. Now bugger off."

The guy switched to Italian and they barked at each other like a couple of angry terriers. Then Frank grabbed the door handle, lurching in his seat like he intended to jump from the car. The young hoodlum straightened up and left in a hurry before Frank rolled up the window.

"Who was that character?"

Frank was still steamed, red-faced and scowling. He dug a pack of Buckinghams from his jacket pocket and fired one up, which seemed to settle him. "That little turd was Johnny Papalia; his old man's Tony, a long-time member of Rocco Perri's old gang who's now with Tedesco. Young Johnny's just getting into the family business. I hear he's peddling drugs in Toronto now."

"What did he say to you in Italian?"

"You don't want to know. It had to do with the rearrangement of some parts of my anatomy."

He started the car and shifted into first gear with a grunt, "Let's get the hell out of here."

CHAPTER FIFTEEN

FRANK WAS LEANING BACK IN his seat and puffing on his cigarette when he turned left onto Plains Road and headed back to town. "Tell me more about Tedesco's so-called retirement."

"She didn't give me any details, just said he was out of favour with Magaddino and was being replaced because of 'certain excesses'. My guess is the big bosses weren't too thrilled by the news coverage of that gory murder of the City Controller. And now the disposal of Bernie's body at my place. But who knows? Maybe he's been holding back on payments to the grand poobah in Buffalo."

"You're right about that publicity; it sure wouldn't help his cause. Having one of his thugs butcher a public official is just plain nuts. Is that all she talked about?"

"Not quite. She and Isabel spoke about her position as the financial brains of the Florida Mob, much as Bessie Starkman was in the Perri gang. She told us they're laundering their money through the real estate market down there –"

"Yeah, yeah. But what the hell is she *doing* up here?"

"Well, she sort of glossed over that part. Didn't want to get into details. But it sounded to me like she's here to get a handle on Tedesco's finances and maybe take the lead in his removal too. You said you remembered her, huh?"

"Of course I do. I was about twelve or so when she left. No offence, but I can still picture her as a real hubba-hubba babe. The teen-age guys would whistle at her when they saw her on the street. And she used to flirt with them when she strolled by – give them a real show."

I pictured my mother swiveling her Dorothy Lamour hips past a gang of juveniles with a toss of her long black hair and a come-along look in her eyes. It wasn't a picture I wanted to see and I shivered it away.

Frank cut his speed as we curved past Dundurn Castle, and along York Street where the traffic slowed to a crawl toward downtown.

"Another thing, Frank. She advised Isabel and me to be careful because Tedesco was still holding a grudge against us. And he might try to retaliate before he retires."

He shot me a sideways glance. "Sounds like pretty good advice but I don't suppose you'll follow it."

I ignored his remark and changed the subject. "I'm wondering about Magaddino. When did he take control of the Ontario gangs?"

"It was while you were still overseas. Remember when you were on the job with the RCMP before the war and how frustrating it was to get a conviction against the Mob bosses? Well, when the war broke out, the Mounties devised a plan to round up all the main Mafia guys when Italy entered the fray. They drew up a list of suspected enemy aliens and subversives, so when Mussolini declared war in May of 1940 –"

"Wait a minute – what do you mean by 'subversives'?"

"It's one of those catch-all terms. After Mussolini teamed up with Hitler, the Mounties' list included all the left-wing agitators they knew about, as well as fascists and their sympathizers. But they also included known members of the Mafia in that list, most of them of Italian background, and the government in Ottawa approved it. As a result, Rocco Perri and his main henchmen, Frank Sylvestro, Tony Papalia, Charlie Bordonaro – that whole shiteree, was interned in Camp Petawawa."

"Hold on, Frank. The government couldn't intern them just because they were Italian. Most of those guys were probably Canadian citizens."

"I know, but here's the thing: being a member of the Mafia and an associate of racketeers and criminals was reason enough to be locked up under the War Measures Act, whether you were a citizen or not. So hundreds of Italians were scooped up from across Canada, most of them here in Southern Ontario."

"And that's when Magaddino –"

"You've got it." We'd stopped at the traffic light on the corner of Queen Street and he turned toward me. "Magaddino and his guys swooped in to take over the remains of Rocco's gang. And he's been in control ever since."

"Why didn't Perri come back to Hamilton after his internment, to pick up where he left off?"

"Well, he sure as hell tried, didn't he? He was released after Italy broke with Germany, sometime toward the end of '43. But the guys in charge were loyal to Magaddino by then and, according to the Mounties, that's when Rocco got his one-way ticket to Burlington Bay."

Frank swung over to King Street and pulled up in front of my office. "Something else I'm curious about," I said. "What does the FBI think my mother's doing up here?"

He glanced toward me. "Magaddino's a very powerful guy; he's got connections everywhere in the U.S. and Canada; one of his cousins is Joe Bananno, head of one of the five crime families in New York City. Another cousin is Guido Tataglia in Miami and they said he's your mother's boss. So they're thinking that Magaddino wanted a 'specialist' to deal with the out-of-control situation here in Hamilton. Someone who could get a handle on the business end of the operation, then arrange an orderly takeover for the next boss. And your mother has the experience, plus she was born and raised right here in Hamilton, so ..."

He might have been describing a group of legitimate businessmen discussing plans to acquire a rival company. The type of arrangement I imagined those tycoons in Toronto made every day in their skyscrapers on Bay Street. How different were they from these gangsters, I wondered, apart from actually murdering their enemies?

"You make it sound like a routine business transaction, Frank. Magaddino calls Tataglia in Miami and orders up someone to clean house in Hamilton."

"Because that's what it is. And your mother fills the bill. We were told that she's not only the accountant for the Mob down there, just like she told you – but she's Tataglia's right-hand woman, if you know what I mean."

I let that sink in, knowing what he meant but not wanting to accept it. "So she's not limited to the finances. Is that what you're saying, Frank?"

He leaned toward me with hooded eyes. "That's exactly what I'm saying."

I'd known deep-down that might be the real purpose of Diane Black's presence here. But it pained me to hear it officially confirmed, and Frank remained quiet as it lodged in my brain like a tumour.

My mother, a Certified Public Accountant, a real estate mogul – and an executioner.

"So what happens now? Will the Hamilton cops do anything to protect Tedesco?"

He humphed. "Majority of the voting public says let the buggers shoot each other; it'll save the taxpayers the cost of housing them in prison. But you know we can't do that – not that we wouldn't like to." He drew in a long breath then sighed. "So we'll do what we always do – try to keep the mayhem down to a minimum and protect the public."

Frank remained silent while I dithered about delivering Diane Black's proposition to him, but I couldn't put it off any longer.

"My mother asked me to deliver a message to Russo, my police friend."

He didn't respond right away, maybe astonished that she'd even remembered him and knew that he was now a cop. "Well, this ought to be good. What's the message?"

"She wants you to convince the police brass to back off for 24 hours while the Mob finishes settling accounts here. She says that police interference will only put the public at risk."

"Hah! Not a chance, Max. Why would she even think I'd agree to that?"

I leaned toward him and lowered my voice. "She knows all about you, Frank: your wife, your kids and your salary – even the amount of your mortgage. So she offered a 'Christmas bonus' if you agreed to delay."

"What?"

"A little something to help with your mortgage."

"That's crazy. What kind of bonus?"

"Five grand."

His breath came out in a soft whistle, then he said, "Holy shitsky."

CHAPTER SIXTEEN

WHEN I RETURNED TO MY office Phyllis waved me over to her desk where she was working on her Barbara Ann Scott scrap book. "Just look at this swell picture, Max. It was in last night's *Spec.*" She was sticking the photo onto a new page with a stubby bottle of LePage's glue.

"All right if I take off my hat and coat first?"

She blushed. "Oh, sure. Here, let me give you a hand." She bustled over to take my coat, then I had a gander at her picture.

She used the eraser end of her pencil as a pointer. "That's the Governor General, Viscount Alexander, and he's presenting Barbara Ann with the medal for the National Amateur Athletic Award for 1947."

"Looks like they're in a hockey rink."

"Yep." She set the pencil aside and continued to smooth the photo into place, blotting up the extra glue with a Kleenex. "Barbara Ann skated a short program during the intermission of an exhibition hockey game in Ottawa with our Olympic team. Of course, you must know that she already holds the Canadian Ladies' Championship and the World Championship Titles for this year."

"Oh, of course."

"The only title remaining is the Olympic gold medal and I can hardly wait. I'm just bustin' my buttons."

I couldn't help admiring her enthusiasm. "I sure hope you're right, Phyl."

Isabel was watching this performance with a shake of her head, then joined me in my office. "I didn't realize you were such a big Barbara Ann fan, Max."

"She'd better win that gold medal – for Phyllis's sake."

We sat at the long table by the wall where I was pleased to see two brown paper bags and a tall carafe of coffee from the White Spot.

Iz poured two cups, unwrapped an egg salad sandwich on brown from one of the bags and fixed me with a stern look. "The funeral, Max. And don't leave anything out."

Contrary to instructions, I gave her a quick summary, then reached for the other bag: a gooey meatball sandwich – my favourite.

"Frank wasn't shocked at what your mother told us about Tedesco's so-called retirement?"

I shook my head and swallowed some coffee. "Nope. The FBI already had Diane Black on their radar in connection with the Florida Mob's activities, so when she travelled up here they informed the RCMP who contacted the Hamilton Police to keep tabs on her. At the cemetery Frank's crew took pictures of the high rollers from out of town."

"But what about that big bribe she wants to offer him. What did he say to that?"

"He was tongue-tied for a minute, probably enjoying a quick fantasy about paying off his mortgage. But you know Frank, he's a straight-shooter. And he had some choice words about what she could do with her offer."

While we ate I gave her more details about Magaddino's mobsters who were in town for the change of command ceremonies, especially the star of the show, Freddy the Wolf.

She gathered up the waxed paper wrappers after we'd eaten and poured more coffee. "I don't get it, Max. Are you saying there's nothing the police can do?"

"Well, they know that Tedesco's on his way out. And they know who's in town to show him the door. But they don't know when and where it'll happen. Their main concern is to protect the public."

"Did you speak to your mother at the cemetery?"

"No. We were trying to be inconspicuous, watching the players through binoculars."

She reached for my hand and gripped it. "But she might be in danger, Max. She's right in the middle of this mess."

I was touched by her concern, but I shook my head. "Diane Black has chosen her own path. There's nothing I can do about that."

After lunch, Isabel stood in the doorway, dressed for winter. "I'm on my way, Max. Meeting with Emma at her office in the Pigott Building at 1:30."

"Still on that bank case?"

"That's right. The police have charged the assistant manager at The Bank of Commerce with embezzling funds. And Emma's going to have a devil of a time defending him."

"Anything you can do?"

"Yes, I hope so. The bank has finally delivered her a copy of the records, which they claim prove the man is guilty. I hope to find something in them that she can use in her client's defence. I'll be there most of the afternoon but I should be back before 5:00."

After she left I called Dave at Veterans' Cab. "Still on duty?"

"Just off the clock, Max. Are we going for another jaunt?"

"Yeah. Can you pick me up outside Birks Jewellers in twenty minutes?"

"Pretty ritzy joint for you. You win the Irish Sweepstakes or something?

"No such luck. But I'll be somewhere else nearby and it's easier to meet you there. I'll be at the curb on the King Street side."

I cut through Gore Park and was standing at Birks jewellery counter 5 minutes later. When I'd passed by here a couple of days ago I'd noticed a fanciful display of diamond rings in the window. But I didn't have time to go in then.

Now, I was approached by a middle-aged woman wearing a sedate black dress with a starched white collar that matched her manner. She stood tall behind her counter inspecting me, maybe wondering if I had the do-re-mi to be taking up her precious time. "I saw the diamond rings in the window," I said, "but the prices weren't shown."

She gave me a wintry smile. "They start at $199."

I caught my breath and wondered about making a discreet escape. "Ah, what about some earrings with a smaller diamond in them?"

She bent down and brought out a tray of diamond earrings from under the counter and set them before me. "Starting from your left they go up in size and also in price. The first pair contain a small diamond chip, but you're in luck, they're on sale for only $79."

I bent over to have a closer look but I could hardly see that chip. "Well ... they're not bad but I was hoping to get something more ... substantial for all that money. You know, when she unwraps it and sees that little blue box with the Birks name on it, she'll be expecting something really nifty."

Her nose tilted upward and she sniffed, "Yes, nothing says quality better than our distinctive blue box, does it?"

I leaned across the counter and lowered my voice. "How about 50 bucks for those earrings?"

"Birks doesn't haggle over prices, Sir."

"Well, in that case, I might just have to take my business elsewhere."

I saw the slightest movement of her thin lips which might've passed for a smile. "I was hoping you'd say that."

Our eyes locked for a few more seconds as I buttoned up my coat and looked quickly around to ensure we wouldn't be overheard. "Say, I was just wondering, you wouldn't be able to sell me an empty box, would you? A couple of bucks?"

Her thin lips whitened as she pinched them together and she backed away from me as though I'd made a lewd comment. Then she pointed to the door and I scooted out of there.

CHAPTER SEVENTEEN

DAVE WAS WAITING AT THE curb when I made my escape from Birk's. I slid in beside him, expecting to be given the third degree because he'd seen me hustling from its main entrance. But he didn't ask and I didn't tell.

While we drove east on Main Street I explained my mission this afternoon to investigate that dog fighting complaint. "Mr. Neatby is the SPCA's lawyer," I said, "and he wants me to take a look at the setup out there; talk to a few neighbours; see what I can learn about this guy and how he operates."

"But if the cops haven't been able to arrest him, what the hell can you do about it?"

I leaned across the seat and clipped him on the arm. "You're doubting the ability of the ace detective, Bud? I'm surprised at you."

He remained quiet until we crossed Kenilworth Avenue where he pulled over at the curb. It was unusual for him not to be jabbering about this or that, so I wondered what was on his mind. He fidgeted in his seat, glancing at me and then turning away. After a long pause, he said, "I know about dog fighting, Max."

"What?" I shifted in my seat to face him and he stumbled over his words at first, then began again.

"I attended one of those fights when I was overseas. Remember when a lot of us Canadians were stuck in the south of England on training and garrison duty for the first couple of years of the war? We were just itching to cross the channel and get into battle. Guys in my unit were bored and anxious and one weekend a couple of the Brits told us about these dog fights they planned to attend. A few of us tagged along with them. And it was brutal, Max. I had to leave after the first fight when the loser was torn to smithereens – I hustled out behind this abandoned farm building where the fights were held and I puked my guts out."

He was staring straight ahead now and the set of his jaw and the twitch of his facial muscles told me he was back behind that building again.

"I've seen photos, Dave. And they were bad enough."

It took him a moment to pull himself together. "Okay, let's have a look at this place. You said somewhere on Parkdale Avenue, right?"

This area was at the edge of the city; a few small houses, a tire repair shop, a couple of garages and a sprawling scrap yard. He made a left turn on Parkdale and headed toward the harbour. "A bit more snow out here than downtown," he said. "And the houses are few and far between, eh?"

"And they're only on the left side of the road," I said.

He pointed toward the open expanse on our right, snow-covered except for two long cleared strips which crisscrossed at the far end. "That's the Municipal Airport on the other side. Ever been in there, Max?"

"Nope. I thought it was closed when the new airport opened at Mount Hope."

He slowed the cab as we watched a twin-engine plane coming in low for a landing, almost on top of us. I had to raise my voice above the roar of the aircraft, "Obviously I was wrong."

"Yeah, it's still a going concern here. Some of the big companies still fly their execs back and forth in their private planes. There's also a regular transport and mail service. And the Hamilton Aero Club flies here; it's a recreational group, and they provide flight training too."

I watched the aircraft land with a bump, then taxi toward a low building off in the distance. "How big's this airport?"

"This is the western boundary. It runs north to Barton Street, then all the way east to the ravine. Couple hundred acres, I think."

"You seem to know a lot about this place, Dave. How come?"

He grunted out a laugh. "My old man was crazy about aviation. This airport was built in '29 and he used to bring me out here when I was a teenager. We'd watch the old biplanes taking off and landing. And there were blimps here as well. We went for a flight over the bay one time and it scared the hell out of me. That's why I signed up for the infantry instead of the Air Force."

"Oh yeah? And I suppose it was a helluva lot safer on that beach at Dieppe, eh?"

"Don't get me going on that, Max. That was one big snafu from beginning to end. The Rileys lost a lot of good men that day. And I consider myself lucky that I only came away with this."

He held up his left hand and I saw for the first time that he was missing his last two fingers.

"Damn good thing I'm right-handed," he said.

I kicked myself in the pants for being unaware of his injury. I felt like a jerk. "Jeez, Dave, I've never noticed because it doesn't seem to bother you. I'm sorry."

"No need. I'm used to it now and you're right – it doesn't hold me back much. Had to give up my career as a concert pianist though."

I shook my head at his black humour. He had the kind of grit that set the RHLI guys apart from other soldiers I'd met – it was an attitude they wore like a badge.

"City of Hamilton owns this airport land," he said, "and I read in *The Spec* that operations will be relocated to Mount Hope in the next couple years. Then this land will be used for a veterans' housing development."

There were fewer than a dozen houses spread out along this stretch and one or two appeared to be abandoned. "Pull over there, Dave, near that white frame place."

He stopped by the side of the road but kept the engine running.

"I don't see a car or truck around," I said. "And that looks like a small barn at the far end of the driveway."

He twisted around in his seat for a better view. "Yeah, and see that wire fencing? Could be kennels in there and maybe a dog-run. Want me to drive in so we can look around?"

"Hell, no. This guy isn't likely to appreciate citizens dropping in uninvited, especially if he's connected to the Mob. Let's stop at the neighbour's just down the road there."

He continued on toward the bay another hundred yards then he followed the tire-tracks into the driveway and pulled in behind a tired 1930's Dodge with a broken tail light. It was parked beside a small bungalow, yellowed strips of paint peeling off its wood siding and I noticed the curtain over the living room window twitching.

I left Dave in the cab and made my way up the cleared path to the door. I had to tug my overcoat tighter against the brisk wind sweeping in off the Bay. I was about to knock when the door was opened by a young woman with a fingertip to her lips. Her hair was done up in curlers covered by a red bandana with white polka dots.

"Shhh, baby's finally gone to sleep." Then she waved me in and closed the door quietly, waiting for me to speak my piece.

I stood on the black rubber floor mat, introduced myself, and passed her one of my cards. "I'm looking into a matter on behalf of the Humane Society. I wonder if you might've heard anything about organized dog fights in this neighbourhood."

She took a step back, inspecting me from head to toe and I must have passed muster because she pointed my card toward the rear of the house. "We can talk in the kitchen."

I stepped out of my toe rubbers and slipped off my coat, then followed her through a small, dim living room: a faded red chesterfield and matching chair faced the window where the curtain remained closed; covering the floor was a worn-out square of linoleum curling at its edges. In one corner a black coal stove was working overtime, its exhaust pipe vented through the ceiling. In the opposite corner stood a four-foot Christmas tree trimmed with candy canes and home-made decorations, a tin-foil star on top.

I followed her into the kitchen where a young girl with pigtails knelt on her chair at the wooden table colouring intently in a picture-book, the tip of her tongue almost touching her nose. The room was neat and clean: ice box in the corner, stove and sink against the far wall. A curling photo of last month's Royal Wedding had been clipped from the newspaper and pinned on the wall beside the telephone.

"My name is Gillian Robertson." She spoke with a British accent which I hadn't detected while she was whispering at the front door. "We haven't lived here long so I'm afraid I don't know the neighbours well. But sit down and we can chat a bit."

"I couldn't help noticing your accent – are you a war-bride?"

I caught a twitch at the corner of her mouth as she looked me in the eye. "That's funny – I thought you spoke like a Yank."

I smiled back and thought we might be off to a good start.

When I sat beside the girl, I pointed at her picture of Santa and his reindeer. "Looks like you're an expert with those crayons, Little Lady. What's your name?"

She darted her eyes at her mother, who nodded. "Nancy. I'm five years old. And I'm going to school next year."

Her mother placed the crayons back in their box and smoothed the girl's unruly hair, "Finish your picture in your room, Lovey. I have to speak to this man for a minute. And don't wake up your father."

The girl scampered away and her mother sat across from me. "Nancy was born in England where I met my hubby, Ben, who was in the RCAF. And the baby, Paula, she was born right here in Hamilton and she's a little sweetheart. Ben's on nights now at Dofasco so I try to keep the children's ruckus down during the day when he's sleeping."

She leaned toward me, getting down to business. "So, you work for the SPCA?"

"Not directly, no. But I'm here on their behalf. The Society was notified by the police that they'd investigated a complaint from someone along your road involving cruelty to dogs. When I saw that house and outbuilding next door I wondered if that might be the place. Would you know anything about that?"

She didn't answer right away but the twitch of her eyes and her pinched mouth told me she knew about it but was reluctant to talk. So I kept my lip firmly buttoned and waited. It was a lesson I'd learned from one of my old instructors in the RCMP – "Just keep your damn trap shut, Dexter," he'd said. "People will always fill the vacuum – eventually."

It took a moment before she spoke. "Yes, I called the police about our next door neighbour. He lives alone there: a grumpy man. I'd guess he's in his fifties or so and he's quite ... rude. We've often heard his dogs barking, usually during the day but sometimes at night, too. When my husband talked to him about it, the man said that's what dogs do – they bark. And it wasn't in his power to change Mother Nature."

I leaned forward in my chair, the concerned listener with his eyebrows raised.

"We had a problem about six or seven weeks ago," she said. "Late one night I heard the dogs making a terrible racket, yelping like I'd never heard before. It woke me up and I could see quite a few cars parked in his long drive, and along the roadside too. Ben was at work so I finally called the police – but when they arrived some time later those cars had already gone. Honestly, it was almost like someone had tipped them off and they all scarpered."

"Then what happened?"

She wagged her head. "The following day I spoke to the sergeant at the station and he said they'd found no evidence of illegal activity. So they gave him a warning to keep the noise down."

Her eyes were downcast when she finished speaking.

"Any more incidents since then?"

"Well, my husband went over to talk to the man again, his name is Grunchy or some name like that. And he told Ben to mind his own business and if the dogs bothered him so much, maybe he should move."

"That seems pretty extreme. What did your husband do?"

"Well, Ben is a big strong man and so is that neighbour, but they didn't fight or anything like that. My husband just told him to keep the noise down or we'd call the police."

"And then?"

"We're not hearing the dogs as much now because we keep the house closed up in this cold weather. But those cars have been back again. I think there might be something going on in that barn building behind his house."

She left the table and ran some water into an aluminum kettle. "Cuppa? It'll be ready in a jiffy."

"Yes, please."

When she returned I asked her, "What about the other neighbours? Are they bothered by these dogs or the owner?"

"You must have noticed we don't have many neighbours out here. I guess people don't want to live this close to the airport. But the rent's cheap and that's important because we're saving up for a place of our own. There's an old couple lives down toward the bay, past that vacant house between us. They're nice folks. They're quiet and keep to themselves and they've never mentioned hearing those dogs. There's another house further down but we don't know those people. We just moved here about six months ago."

"What about in the other direction – toward Main Street?"

She rose from the table and poured the boiling water into a fat brown teapot. "Well, let's see. Up at the corner of Dunsmure Road there's a nice young family, four children; we visited them a few times during the summer – the Kellams. Across the street from them, so they told us, there's a cranky old woman who's always chasing the kids off her property when they cut through on their way to school. Mrs. Kellam warned me she's quite the busybody, listens in on the party line all the time, but I've never noticed that. Mind you, I don't use the phone a lot. And that old woman is related somehow to our neighbour with the dogs. As I said, we haven't lived here long so that's all I know about the neighbours."

She went on to tell me about her difficult time in England during the war while we drank our tea. When she'd run out of steam, I thanked her for her time and as we shook hands at the doorway she said, "Oh, I almost forgot. We have a newspaper lad who makes the rounds out here. He's sure to know more about the neighbours than I do. Just a minute and I'll get his name for you."

In the kitchen, she riffled through a drawer beside the sink. Then she bustled back to the doorway, waving a *Spectator* punch card. "His name's Trevor. There's his address on Dunsmure and the phone number."

I scribbled the information from the card into my notebook. "Do you mind giving me your number, in case I have to follow up about anything?"

I made a note of it, then put on my coat, hat and rubbers. "Your neighbour could be involved in staging dog-fights and that's a criminal offence. So if you hear another disturbance next door, or see something unusual, be sure to call the police again."

"I will," she said. "And thanks ever so."

CHAPTER EIGHTEEN

DAVE HAD THE ENGINE RUNNING and the heater on high as I slid in beside him. He was staring straight ahead and I thought he might be upset about my delay.

"Sorry I was so long, Dave, but the woman was chatty. You were right about the next-door neighbour. He's keeping dogs in that low building behind his house. And she called the cops about a commotion over there a while ago – cars coming and going late at night, a lot of noise. But by the time they arrived, everyone but the owner had gone."

Dave's eyes were jittery when he finally looked up at me. And when he started to speak his voice croaked so he began again. "Something just happened."

"C'mon, Dave. Spit it out – was is it?"

"Well … while I was waiting, I started to get antsy and got out to look around. I knew you might be a little while so I snuck over to that place next door. I approached from the back so the guy wouldn't see me if he was home. We didn't notice his car from the road because his garage is out back there, on the other side of the dog kennels. He's got a truck, too. So when I came around the corner of the house this big arm reached out and caught me by the throat. Took me completely by surprise, Max. And he damn near strangled me."

"Dammit, Dave. I told you that bird might be connected to the Mob. How'd you get away?"

"I had to talk fast, that's for damn sure. Told him I was visiting a friend next door and thought I heard dogs barking, sounding they like might need help and it didn't look like anyone was home. So I was just being a good Samaritan, going to help the dogs."

"Oh, jeez. Don't tell me he fell for that line."

"Well, yeah, he did. Damn good thing for me that he's not too bright. I finally convinced him to let me go and I got back to my cab in double quick time. No harm done, except that I feel like such a dope."

I delivered a light punch to his right arm. "I'm glad you didn't get hurt, Bud. You'll believe me next time, right?"

"Roger that."

He had the look of a guy who'd just been yanked out of Lake Ontario in sub-zero weather. "I don't suppose you heard me when I told you about the woman next door calling the cops, etcetera?"

Dave shook his head. So I repeated her story.

"Shit. Sounds like he might've gotten a warning that the cops were on the way."

"Sure does, doesn't it? Now let's get the hell out of here."

I asked Dave to turn right at the corner of Dunsmure, the street where the newspaper carrier lived. He slowed as he turned off Parkdale and I had a good look at the house on the corner belonging to the cranky old lady – it was a two-storey frame building, showing its age, perhaps like its owner. Across the corner of her lot, I made out a footpath tramped into the snow, evidence of the kids' short-cut to school. I didn't notice her peeking out from behind her curtains, wondering what a taxicab was doing out here so I guessed she was only a part-time busybody.

In the next block, we pulled over at the curb. "Sure this is the right number, Max? This place looks way too small for a family."

"It's the address she gave me. But I'll find out quick enough, won't I?"

The walkway had been neatly cleared; a snow shovel and an old broom were propped up beside the front entrance. I rapped on the door. No answer. Rapped again, much harder.

The door opened a crack and a beady eye gave me the once-over. "What do you want, Mister?"

That eye was at the level of my neck and the voice had that breaking quality you hear in teenage boys. I smiled to myself, remembering my own embarrassment during that awkward phase.

I stuck my business card through the small opening and spoke in a hoarse, on-the-sly whisper. "I'm a private eye following up on a case where you deliver newspapers and maybe you can help me. One of your customers told me where you lived. So your name's Trevor, eh?"

He snapped the card from my fingers, read it, then flung the door open wide, banging it against the wall. "That's me, Mister. C'mon in. So you're hot on the trail of some bad guys, eh?"

I got a kick out of his enthusiasm and closed the door behind me as I stepped into the living room. The kid was about thirteen or so, as skinny as that broom handle beside the doorway, with a mop of dark hair above his pimply face. I made a quick scan of the room: a couple of old upholstered chairs and an ugly green couch, sagging in the middle like a swayback horse. The carpet had seen better days but the house was clean; someone was making an effort to make the place livable. An ancient radio console dominated one corner, a police siren wailing from its speaker, followed by gunshots. And a smaller boy, about seven or eight, lay on the floor in front of the radio, his chin cradled on his palms, absorbed in today's spine-tingling episode of Dick Tracy or some other crime buster. He turned toward me as I entered then shot a wary glance at his big brother, who gave him a nod of approval.

"Your mother or father at home?"

"Nope, my mum works 'til six. And my dad ... never came back from the war. So there's just me and my kid brother here. Now what about these bad guys? What did they do? How can I help?"

"Just hold your horses, Bud. Can we go through to the kitchen and talk?"

"Sure."

I followed him into the kitchen which was also spic and span: an old-style electric range beside the sink and a wooden ice-box against the back wall. I noted with approval that Trevor had closed the kitchen door behind us rather than telling his kid brother to turn down the radio. You can't listen properly to cops and robbers at low volume.

We sat at a red arborite table with chrome legs and matching chairs and the kid pushed his school books and some note paper aside. "I'll finish my homework later. This is more important."

I nodded my head, recalling my own school days when I'd latch onto any excuse to delay doing my homework. Then I got back to business: "You deliver along Parkdale, right? Beside the airport?"

"Yep. I've got 31 customers. Along Dunsmure here, up to Kenilworth, then over to Main Street and back along Parkdale beside the airport."

I leaned toward him and lowered my voice. "There's a guy who keeps some dogs out behind his house on Parkdale. You know the place?"

"You bet. But he doesn't take the paper. People next door do, the Robertsons."

"Did you ever look around his place, see him with his dogs?"

"Sure, I've seen him sometimes. But he's a mean guy – if he ever sees you hanging around his property he chases you away. Why're you asking – did he do something wrong?"

"I don't know yet. That old woman who lives at the corner – someone told me she might be related to that guy."

"Yeah, she's his mother. Mean old witch, always complaining about the paper being late or yelling at me for cutting across her property. And I have to fold up the paper so it fits in this dinky little milk box at her side door. She's always telling me to speak up 'cuz she says she's deaf – but I see her on the phone all the time."

I recalled Mrs. Robertson telling me she was an eavesdropper.

"How do you know she's this guy's mother?"

"She told me that when I took over this route last year. Said her son picks up her paper after she's read it – the cheapskate."

"What's his name?"

"She calls him Sonny but I don't know his real first name. His last name's probably the same as hers, and that's Gruchy. But I call her 'Grouchy' 'cuz that's what she is. One Saturday when I was collecting she's counting out the exact change from this little green purse she keeps in her apron and I said under my breath, 'Don't give me one extra penny, Mrs. Grouchy' and she says right away, 'What did you call me?' So she sure ain't deaf."

I liked this kid. He was observant and spoke right up. "What about her son's place – do you see lots of visitors down there, cars coming and going?"

"Nah, it's usually quiet. Except for the dogs. 'Course, I'm only down there once a day after school with my papers. And on Saturday afternoons when I do my collecting. Couple times I saw a delivery guy dropping off big sacks of stuff – could've been dog food, I guess."

"Did you ever speak with this Gruchy guy?"

"Nope, but he scared the heck out of me a couple times; I remember once I was hiding in them bushes beside the pens, watching him with his dogs. He's got this contraption like a conveyor belt and the dogs run on it while he speeds it up and they have to run faster and faster or they get thrown off, see? So I was looking at this one dog running like blue blazes then he was tossed right off and hit the wall, yelping and barking. I must've called out or made a noise 'cuz the guy saw me and nearly caught me when I took off. He used some pretty bad language, too."

"Did you ever figure out what he was doing?"

"I think he's training them to be hunting dogs 'cuz they could sure run hard."

I stashed my notebook in my jacket pocket and got up from the table. "Well, thanks for your help, Trevor. But from now on I think you should be careful around this Gruchy guy, he could be dangerous. We got a deal?" And I stuck out my hand.

He shook it like the man of the house. "Sure thing, Mister. And if I see anything suspicious I'll phone this number on your card."

Walking to the door, I noticed there was no Christmas tree or decorations, which seemed unusual so close to Christmas. "You wait for Christmas Eve to put up your tree?"

"Nah, my mum doesn't bother since my dad's not here. She always says, 'Maybe next year'."

I dug out my wallet and withdrew a $5 bill. "Here," and I passed it to him. "You and your brother could surprise her with a nice Christmas present."

CHAPTER NINETEEN

DAVE FLICKED OFF THE RADIO and turned toward me as I slid onto the front seat of the cab beside him. "How did it go with the paperboy? Any help?"

"Yeah, he's a sharp kid. He's seen that guy training his animals and figures he's raising them as hunting dogs because he saw them running on some kind of conveyor belt gizmo."

I heard him catch his breath as he shifted his eyes away from me and stared out the window. "Trainers use a treadmill rig like that to strengthen the dogs' stamina and develop their muscles."

His voice was strained, as though someone was squeezing his neck. "My Brit friend told me they also chain their dogs to a merry-go-round thingamajig which increases in speed – the dogs try to catch a chunk of meat dangling in front of them but of course, they can never get the bait. And sometime the dogs are hung by their jaws to strengthen their biting power. It's an ugly business, Max."

I was holding my breath while he spoke, disgusted with sadistic morons who'd torture their animals like that. But I was determined to hear the rest of it. "Tell me about the fight itself, Dave. How did that work?"

I saw the grimace on his face and almost stopped him from speaking. But I didn't – my damn curiosity again.

"The fight I saw was in a barn way off in the countryside. The bettors were crowded around a penned-off area about fifteen feet square, low wooden walls three or four feet high, and the floorboards were covered with a rough carpeting. To improve the dogs' traction.

"The two handlers brought their dogs to the centre of the pit where the referee watched as they exchanged their dogs then returned to their corners and washed them off –"

"Wait a minute. Why would the handlers wash each other's dogs?"

"I asked about that too. Some shifty dog owners were known to rub a noxious substance on their dogs which would paralyze their opponents when they were bitten. So, after the washing, the dogs and the handlers returned to the middle with the referee who said, 'Face your dogs' followed by 'Go!' Then the dogs wrestled and snarled, biting each other and trying to get a 'turn' – that's when one of the mutts turns away from the other and stops fighting."

"So that's when the fight ends? When one of the dogs quits?"

"No, not yet. Then the ref orders the dogs back to their corners where the handlers wash the blood off them and patch them up if they can. When the ref calls 'Time' the dogs must come out to what's called the 'scratch line', that's a line marked on the centre of the floor; then they continue to fight. If a dog fails to cross the scratch line and won't fight, he loses the match. But if he does cross the line, the fight resumes until one of the dogs gives up or dies."

"My God. How long does a fight last?"

"The guy told me it often goes on for an hour or more. But I didn't last that long. I had to get the hell out of there when I felt my stomach heaving."

Those pictures Mr. Neatby had shown me had nearly made me sick; listening to what Dave had witnessed brought me to the brink again.

We didn't speak on the return trip until he dropped me off. "See you, Max."

"Yeah, thanks."

Back in my office, I slipped off my coat and hung it up. Phyllis was busy typing but Isabel was quick to notice the sombre look on my face and she grasped my arm when I skirted her desk.

"Hang on, Max. What's happened?"

I nodded toward my office. She followed me in and closed the door.

"Dave and I drove out to the east end, beside the Civic Airport. I think we found the property where those dog fights are taking place and I talked to a neighbour about it."

I gave her a slightly edited version of what I'd learned from Mrs. Robertson and from Dave about the dog fight he'd witnessed, which accounted for my gloomy frame of mind.

We sat at the long table by the window; Isabel clutched my hands and remained silent in the wake of my report. Then she shook her head. "For the life of me, Max, I can't understand why people would enjoy watching animals fight and die. It's just ... barbaric – something from the Middle Ages."

"That's why I'd like to help put these guys out of business. After I left the neighbour's place I met with *The Spectator* carrier out there and he gave me the low-down on a few of the neighbours."

I related the kid's story about his close call while watching the owner training his dogs. And his troubles with the old lady who was the owner's mother. "I'm getting an idea about how to approach this problem, but I'll have to think about it some more."

Isabel stood and ambled toward the doorway; then she slowed and turned back to me. "That neighbour woman wondered if the dog owner might have been warned about the police coming, is that right?"

"Yep."

"And the houses out there are on a party-line?"

"That's what she told me."

"Well, maybe the old lady on the corner tipped off her son. The newspaper boy figured out she wasn't deaf so she could've been up late. Lots of old people don't sleep well, and maybe she was listening in on the party line for something to do. Those party-lines are notorious for eavesdroppers. So she hears her son's neighbour, Mrs. what's-her-name, calling the police then she warns him. And there you go, Max – Bob's your uncle."

She was standing taller now, pleased with her solution, a sparkle in her eyes.

I didn't want to tell her that I'd already dismissed that theory and I felt my heart sink as she frowned at my non-reaction. It didn't feel good to disappoint her.

She returned to the table and held both my hands in hers. "I'm only trying to help, Max. It's just a possibility you might not have considered because you were so busy out there."

"It's a good idea, Iz. But I didn't pursue it because you always hear a click on a party line if someone else picks up when you're using the phone. And Mrs. Robertson didn't mention hearing an eavesdropper. So I was on a different track; I was thinking that the dog owner might've been tipped off by someone he knew in the police dispatcher's office and I planned to follow that up with Frank."

Her eyes held mine and I hoped she didn't think I'd dismissed her theory simply because she was new to the detective game. A silent moment later, she placed her hand on my shoulder and stood to leave. "Every once in a while in the accounting business," she said, "the simple answer is the correct one."

I thought about her comment as I followed her to the door. "Once in a while in the sleuthing business, the simple answer sails right over my head."

After she left, I called Frank Russo and explained my involvement with the SPCA and my excursion this afternoon to ferret out some info.

"Yeah, we hear about those fights from time to time," he said. "But more often than not it's cock-fighting; I was on a raid in the north end before the war and our main concern was collaring the gangsters there. To be honest, we didn't worry a helluva lot about the dead and wounded roosters. They're only chickens, eh?"

"Come on, Frank, it's against the law. Cruelty to animals – it doesn't matter what kind of animals they are. It's a case of men behaving like savages."

"You tellin' me you don't eat chicken? How do you think it winds up on your dinner plate? Somebody's gotta kill the damn birds."

"I know that but the animals we eat are usually slaughtered humanely. That's a helluva lot different than dogs and roosters which are trained as killers so they can tear each other apart in bloody combat while so-called sportsmen bet on the outcome. Well, that's just plain –"

"Hang on a damn minute, Max. Get down off your high horse and listen. I agree there's a big difference, just as you say. And I know about dog fights and how gory they are. Hell, we've prosecuted a couple of those offenders. But why are you telling me all this? What do you want from me?"

I took a few deep breaths to control my frustration. Frank wasn't the enemy and I hadn't intended to dump my revulsion onto his head like an icy shower. "I'm sorry, Pal. The more I think about this business, the more disgusted I become. I didn't mean to take it out on you."

"Fine. Now, what do you want me to do?"

"Well, this guy out there, Gruchy is his name, he's training these dogs and probably staging fights on his property. Couple of months back, the next-door neighbour called the police to report a commotion at the guy's place, lots of cars and noise. But by the time the cops arrived, the place had cleared out and no arrests were made and no charges laid."

"Someone tipped him off?"

"Sounds like it. And I wondered if it might've been one of the police dispatchers. Maybe this Gruchy guy out there is the dispatcher's brother-in-law or connected in some other way. Do you think that's a possibility?"

I heard him grunt in my ear. "Nope ... couldn't have happened. And not just because the dispatchers are police officers. The sergeant in charge of the Radio Room is a guy by the name of Rod Latner. You know him?"

"Never met him."

"Well, he's a hard-nosed character; one of those spit and polish types who should've been a drill sergeant in the army. He runs a tight ship; those dispatchers can't blow their noses without him knowing about it. He monitors their calls and watches them like they might be stealing the family silver. So I'd forget about that theory."

So much for my brilliant idea. "You're absolutely sure, Frank?"

"I'd bet my life on it. But I'll ask around, see if anyone's picked up any scuttlebutt about this Gruchy guy."

I thanked him, hung up the receiver and sagged back in my chair. Damn, damn and double damn. With that hunch of mine now in the toilet, I wondered if the simple answer might be the right one, just as Iz suggested.

Damn again.

CHAPTER TWENTY

I'D JUST FINISHED MAKING SOME notes on my afternoon trip with Dave when the office door opened. I looked up and stared bug-eyed as Isabel swished toward me like a fashion model and the office became her runway. She wore a silky red dress fitted at her waist then flaring at the hem just below her knees. "That dress is a humdinger, Iz. And the sprig of ivy at the neckline looks nifty with it. Did you just run home to change?"

"No. I brought the dress to the office this morning and changed in the washroom." She twirled so the hem rose a few inches to reveal her knees and I felt my heart skip a beat. "I'm glad you like it, Max. Phyllis gave me the ivy."

It took me a moment to find my voice. "So … ah, what's happening? All dressed up like a million bucks."

"I'm off to the Yuletide Cocktail party put on by the Chartered Accountants Association. It's just across the street at the Connaught this year. I'd ask you to come with me but you'd be bored to tears with all their shop talk."

I breathed a secret sigh of relief. She was getting to know me really well.

"I let Phyllis go early," she said. "She's taking her mother Christmas shopping."

She leaned across my desk and pecked me on the cheek. "See you tomorrow, Boss."

I stowed the files in the bottom drawer of the desk and was putting on my coat in the outer office when I caught a glimpse of myself in the mirror that Phyllis had mounted on the wall beside the filing cabinets. The guy looking back at me wore a rumpled suit, his tie hung loose, and his hair was shaggy. I watched the guy pull a face at himself. Then I pictured him standing beside Isabel in that dazzling red cocktail dress. Holy cow! Why would she be interested in such a messy lout?

I took a deep breath, stood a little taller, combed my hair with my fingers and straightened my tie. I decided to get a haircut.

Mr. Whitmore's barber shop was in the basement of the *Spectator* building so I didn't have far to go. I gripped my way down the steep stairs and saw I was in luck – one of the five barber chairs was open. Along a side wall was a row of tall shoeshine chairs – only two of those were occupied. A discreet sign read: Haircut 50¢ Shoe Shine 15¢.

I liked the comfy atmosphere down here – customers and barbers murmuring about the lousy weather or what to get their wives for Christmas or the soaring cost of living – all to the tune of the scissors' clickety-click and the snapping of the shoeshine rags. And through the two narrow windows set high in the street-side wall, you could see the busy feet of downtown workers and Christmas shoppers hustling along King Street.

Mr. Whitmore was shaving a lathered-up face in the chair beside me and glanced over as I sat down.

"How you doing, Max?" he said. "In for your annual haircut?"

That was Whitmore's stock line whenever I came into his shop. But in fact, I got my hair cut every month or two, whenever I remembered. "I didn't recognize the guy in my bathroom mirror this morning so I knew it was time." That was my usual response and I watched him wince as I delivered it.

A young barber I didn't recognize draped a striped cloth over my suit and cranked the chair down a notch. "How would you like it, Sir? Shorter all round or just a trim?"

I noted the name tag on his white barber's jacket. "Nice and short, Dino. So I won't have to come back so often."

Mr. Whitmore glanced at me with a tiny grin as he rinsed his razor at the sink. He seemed to enjoy our little game.

Now that the face beside me had been shaved I recognized that it belonged to Sam Lawrence, Hamilton's flamboyant Mayor, and he turned toward me.

"Say, aren't you that young fella in the newspaper with the dead body on his porch? What a dreadful shock that must have been. How're you doing?"

That damn photo again – would I never hear the end of it?

"Doing all right, Mr. Mayor. And congratulations on being acclaimed for another term in office. What's that make it now, five years in a row?" Civic elections were held every year on January first. Unless, like this year for Sam Lawrence, he was popular enough that nobody ran against him.

He swiveled his head, a smile on his face. "Well, thank you," and he tugged back the cloth covering his suit so he could stick out his mitt for me to shake. Both barbers had to stop clipping for a moment to make time for this glad-handing.

"That newspaper article suggested the killing was connected to organized crime and this city has more than its share of that," the Mayor said. "That brutal murder of George Harris, Chairman of our Planning Committee, is a case in point."

"It's a problem that seems to defy solution," I said. "How do you think these criminals might be controlled?"

I saw the muscles in his jaw moving as though he were chewing over his answer. "That's a tough question. But I believe the solution is straightforward – we need more police officers on the streets and they deserve to be paid more. I know it's difficult but the City has to keep pace with the cost of living. Why, did you know it's up more than 20% since 1944? We also need better paying jobs for young people entering the work force and that might cut down on the number of young men who now consider joining the Mob because it pays more than an honest job.

"I know, I know, you probably expect me to say that we need more and stronger unions to support workers' rights – and that is true. And I'll keep saying it over and over again until employers treat their people fairly."

It wasn't the time, nor was it the place to warn the Mayor of the mayhem which would accompany the impending gangland struggle so I kept my trap shut on that score.

Mr. Whitmore stood patiently by while His Worship delivered his little speech. As soon as he'd stopped for a breath of air, the barber turned the Mayor's head firmly forward and finished cutting his hair.

Mayor Lawrence heaved himself out of his chair and palmed Mr. Whitmore some money, then he stood still while the barber whisked off the stray hairs from his fashionable double-breasted suit. He put on his overcoat and waved his hat to everyone in the shop. "Happy Christmas to you all."

A kind of vacuum took over the room when the door closed behind him, as though his departure had sucked the energy out of the place.

Mr. Whitmore broke the strange silence. "He's quite the man, Max. Love him or hate him, you know he has the City's best interests at heart."

"I heard he stirred up quite a hornet's nest," I said, "when he marched with the strikers during that big labour dispute last year at Stelco."

A couple of customers mumbled something under their breath.

"That's right," Mr. Whitmore said. "He's been a socialist all his life. But the press had a field day when some reporter was giving him a hard time for joining the picket line and Sam was quoted as saying, 'I'm a union man first and a Mayor second.' So even if you don't agree with him, you have to admit he's got the courage of his convictions."

An old boy in the chair at the end of the row had the last word on the subject. "I think he's a pretty smart guy, that Mayor. He's not like your other politicians – he uses his head for more than a hat-rack."

Leaving the shop I caught sight of a well-groomed guy in the long mirror by the doorway. Jeez, it was me. I was beginning to look more like someone Isabel wouldn't be embarrassed to be seen with.

CHAPTER TWENTY-ONE

W‍HEN I GOT HOME THE phone was ringing. I kicked my toe-rubbers toward the doormat and hurried to the kitchen where I grabbed the receiver.

"Is that Mr. Dexter?" A young voice, midway between soprano and alto.

"Yeah, who's this?" I had one arm out of my overcoat and switched the phone to my other hand.

"It's Trevor. The *Spectator* carrier."

"What's happening, Kid, you in some kind of trouble?"

"Nah. But I said I'd call you if I seen something suspicious."

"I remember. So what did you see?"

"Well, I just delivered the paper to Mrs. Robertson on Parkdale; she's at the end of my route. You know … the lady next door to the guy with the dogs? And when I got closer to that guy's house, well, I seen this truck, some kind of small delivery van and it pulled into his driveway. Then these two guys jumped out and started unloading boxes and stuff, taking them round to that barn behind the house –"

"Wait a minute; slow down. What kind of stuff?"

"It was just getting dark so it was hard to see. But some of those boxes were cases of beer, I could hear the bottles clinking together –"

"Hang on. How do you know what beer bottles sound like?"

"We had our annual bottle drive for the Boy Scouts last week. Some of the people gave us their beer bottles and that's the noise they made."

This kid was one smart cookie.

"I ain't finished yet. So when those guys left in their truck, another one drove in. This time there were three big guys and they brought out these wire cages with dogs in them and carried them out back. I counted them – six cages in all. But I didn't want to get any closer to see what kind of dogs they were."

Sonovabitch. Preparations for dog-fights were underway, probably for tonight. I felt my pulse quicken and my heartbeat shift into a higher gear. "Listen, did any of those guys see you watching them?"

"Nope. I stayed behind those bushes beside the driveway. And it was getting dark by then."

"Good. Now, I want you to stay away from that place. I think there's some kind of criminal activity going on there. Are we agreed on this? Do I have your word?"

"Yeah, sure, Mr. Dexter. But I was going to tell my mum, is that okay?"

"Of course, but nobody else. Is she there now? I'd like to talk to her."

"She's still at work. Stores are open 'til nine o'clock now – right up to Christmas."

"All right, but tell her she can call me if she wants to and I'll explain it to her. Oh, I almost forgot. What's the house number for that guy with the dogs?"

"I'm not sure because he's not a customer. Just look in the phone book."

Then the kid was silent for a few seconds and I wondered if he had more on his mind. "Anything else you wanted to tell me, Trevor?"

"Umm … I just wanted to say thanks again for giving me that money for a present for my mum."

"You're welcome. Did you decide what you're going to get her?"

"Oh, sure. My brother and me are going to Robinson's on the bus tomorrow after papers. We can't go to Eaton's because that's where my mum works and she might see us. We're getting her a Yardley gift set – two bars of Yardley soap and it comes with a small bottle of Yardley perfume."

"Nice gift. How did you come up with that?"

"My Dad used to give her Yardley's at Christmas and on her birthday."

That raised my eyebrows – what a thoughtful kid. "You got enough money for that?"

"Sure do. The gift set's $4.50. And then on the way home we're getting a Christmas tree. This guy over on Main Street sells them for a buck this close to Christmas."

"But that'll leave you ... 50¢ short."

"Nope. My brother and me get 25¢ allowance every month. So we'll chip that in too."

"Sounds like you've got it all figured out, Kid. Thanks for calling me. And Merry Christmas."

I hung up my coat and shucked off my suit jacket and tie. Back in the kitchen, I phoned Frank at home.

"I'm calling about that guy with the fighting dogs I told you about. Out there on Parkdale, across from the Airport?"

"Yeah, yeah, I remember. But can't this wait? We just sat down for supper."

"'Fraid not, Frank, it's an emergency. I just got a call from that newspaper kid I met out there. A few minutes ago he saw some guys delivering crates of dogs to that place on Parkdale, along with booze and other stuff."

I reached for a note on the counter and gave him the guy's address. I'd gotten it from the phone book. "Sounds like they're preparing for dog fights tonight. What d'you say to an early visit from Santa? In the form of a raiding party to catch those buggers red-handed?"

"Helluva good idea. Homicide won't be handling the case, but I'll call the sergeant who'll organize the raid. He might want to speak with you directly so I'll give him your phone number. Thanks for the tip, Max; I'll let you know when I hear something."

I placed a pot of water on the stove to boil and I measured out a big serving of spaghettini. Frank's wife, Angela, kept me supplied with her special tomato sauce and I took out a large jar and set it on the counter beside the pasta.

The phone rang again. I turned off the burner before I answered.

"It's Terry Martin calling from the Hamilton Police Department, Mr. Dexter. Frank Russo gave me your number and I appreciate your help. Maybe you could run through what you told him."

"Sure thing, Sergeant." I gave him a quick summary of my visit this afternoon and the tip-off from the newspaper carrier.

"That's good news," he said. "We know about this bird and he's a slippery bugger. He moved out there to Parkdale Avenue last year – after we'd paid him a visit at a property he was renting near Waterdown. We couldn't charge him for fighting his dogs then because the fights had finished and the crowd dispersed by the time we got there. But he was fined for various liquor offences. Damn law is weak in this area, as you probably know."

"Yeah, I think it's stupid. I hope you catch him in the act this time. Good luck to you."

After supper, I was reading the paper when the phone rang again – I didn't get this many calls at the office. It was Frank.

"News about the raid on the dog guy already?"

He grunted in my ear. "Too early for that. No, I wanted to tell you about my visit to the jail late this afternoon and you were so damn excited when you called before that I forgot all about it. I dropped in on my way home from work and had a talk with Nick Fiore, trying to loosen his tongue about that murder at Paddy Greene's. But he's clammed up tighter than a flea's patootie. I told him what Bernie said to you about Sal Angotti being the actual killer and he denied saying it. He said his brother was never a smart guy and must've been confused. And it surprised me that Nick showed no sign of anger toward his bosses for bumping off his only brother. He's sticking to his story – somebody knocked him out in the parking lot at Greene's and he woke up in jail."

"He knows damn well what happens to jail-house canaries, Frank."

"Yep. That's why he told me not to come back. There ain't no secrets in the joint – especially if a prisoner gets a visit from a copper."

"Did he ask you about the funeral? If you saw his parents?"

"Not a goddamn word. He's a hard guy and his lip is buttoned."

I stayed up as late as I could, but when there was no word on the raid by midnight I decided to hit the sack. I put an extra blanket on the bed because of the predicted cold snap and fell asleep right away.

I don't know how much time had passed when an insistent high-pitched ringing – as loud as an air-raid siren – shocked me out of bed. I was searching my apartment in a frenzy, stumbling like a blind man from room to room, trying to locate its source as it increased in volume. I staggered about, banging into walls, knocking over an end table and then a kitchen chair. I was trying to step over the chair when a bloody arm shot out from under the table and grabbed my ankle, bringing me down with a crash on the kitchen floor where I lay prone and face to face with a sneering German tank commander, his grey jacket crisp and clean and his eyes flashing with fire as he raised his Luger and pressed it against my temple. He counted down, *drei, zwei, eins* … then his head was blown off his shoulders and his blood geysered over me.

I scrambled away from him, groping my way to the front door and into the outstretched arms of Bernie Fiore. He held me in a bear hug, sobbing on my shoulder. I struggled to free myself but my hands slipped off him, covered with blood seeping from the bullet wounds in the back of his head. His lips didn't move but I could hear his accusing words all around me: "You should've helped me, Max, you should've helped me." I tried to run away, but Bernie's arms were cold and tight around my torso.

I woke up in the front hallway, my arms wrapped around the coat rack, tears streaking down my cheeks, as exhausted as a marathon runner stumbling across the finish line. My pajamas were soaked through but that strident ringing had quit, bringing my nightmare to an end.

A moment later the ringing began again. I groped my way to the kitchen, flicked on the light and checked the clock – 0230. Then I answered the phone.

A raspy voice croaked, "Sorry, wrong number."

I'd never heard those words uttered like a threat before. I hung up the phone, tumbled back into bed and worried myself back to my nightmares.

CHAPTER TWENTY-TWO

WHEN I AWOKE IN THE morning the phone was ringing again. I pinched myself to make sure I was awake and not reliving that nightmare. Then I hustled into the kitchen and picked up the receiver, wondering if it might be that "wrong number" voice again.

"Max, it's Frank. What took you so damn long to answer? You sleeping in?"

"Yeah, something like that." I glanced at the wall clock – 0830. "I had a long night."

"Well, we've got some good news for a change. That raid out on Parkdale Avenue worked out tickety-boo. They rounded up a dozen guys; most of them'll be charged with liquor offences and some with possession of unlicensed weapons. But we've got this Gruchy character on keeping a common gaming house, and the unlicensed sale of booze. Some drugs were confiscated, too. And finally, cruelty to animals for staging those fights. The SPCA had their van out there and took away the dead and injured dogs. How's that for a night's work?"

"Pretty damn good, Frank. I'm really glad to hear it."

"Well, it's thanks to you for that tip-off. Good work, Max."

"It wasn't me. That newspaper kid gets the credit for keeping his eyes open and letting me know. He'd be tickled pink if he got a letter or something from the Police Chief. What d'you say?"

"Good idea. I'll look into it and let you know."

We didn't speak for a moment. Frank was waiting for me to continue. He knew me so well that he was able to sense when I had something else on my mind.

"C'mon, Maxie. What's up?"

"Yeah, well, I had this nightmare, that's why I slept in. Bernie Fiore paid me a visit; he was upset with me for not helping him and it became quite ... emotional. When I woke up I got this phone call – a creepy voice saying he'd dialed a wrong number. So I was wondering if there were any Mob guys picked up during the raid."

"Why? You think the Mob's trying to rattle you with wrong-number phone calls because you tipped us off about the dog fights?"

"It's possible, isn't it?"

"Maybe," he said. "But those guys aren't usually that subtle. If they're mad at you – BAM, they hit you. Do you think someone spotted you snooping around out there?"

"I know so. That Gruchy guy warned off my cab driver, Dave Rettig. You might remember him – he served with the Rileys and he's the son of Ted Rettig, that famous sculptor."

Frank mumbled. "Yeah, I remember Dave. But I never heard of his old man."

"Anyway," I said, "while I was in talking with Gruchy's neighbour, Dave snuck around to the back of his house to look the place over. Damned if he didn't get caught and was run off the property. Gave the guy some lame excuse and talked himself out of a beating or worse."

"Seems like a long shot to me, Max. But, yeah, some of the guys arrested were Tedesco's soldiers. I think it's more likely your phone call was just a prank. Or maybe you've got a case of the willies and you dreamed that too."

I grunted at him. "Don't think so. I'll bet Gruchy told one of the Mob guys he had a snooper in a Veterans Cab nosing around in the afternoon. And it's no trick at all for the Mob to squeeze the cab company and find out the name of the driver ... and his fare."

"Yeah ... maybe you're right." There was a long pause on the line. "So just in case, it wouldn't hurt to strap on your gun."

After my bath, I set out my usual breakfast on the kitchen table: a large bowl of Grape-Nuts Flakes, and a cup of Maxwell House. I stepped out on the back porch to get my bottle of milk and there beside the milkbox was – another goddamn body!

This time it was a dead dog, battered and bloodied. One eye had been gouged out and was drooping from its socket in a mucous sac. Around its neck was a red Christmas bow.

If Tedesco was trying to scare the hell out of me, he was on the right track. First Bernie's body, then that creepy phone call and now this mangled animal. But he had no idea about my stubborn streak, probably inherited from that dark-haired and dark-minded woman who was in town to deliver him the Mob's Christmas message.

I stepped inside and found an old sheet in my closet rag-bag to cover the dog's corpse. Then I called Mr. Neatby.

"Just arrived at my office," he said. I could hear the excitement in his voice. "Congratulations on a job well done, Mr. Dexter. I got a call at home early this morning – I certainly didn't expect such a quick result. Criminals arrested, dogs taken in for treatment or burial. It's a banner day for the SPCA and we owe you a big debt."

"Thanks, but it wasn't only me." Then I told him about the paperboy's help. "I'm actually calling about something else." I explained that I'd found a dead dog on my back porch and asked him to arrange for its removal. "I've covered it in an old sheet and I hope it can be taken away discreetly. I don't want to spook the neighbours again."

"Good Grief, that's shocking. And I sincerely apologize for bringing this trouble to your doorstep, Mr. Dexter. I'll look after it right away and –"

He was about to continue when I cut him off. "Please, it wasn't your fault and I don't blame you. We're dealing with people who have no regard for the law. And no qualms at all about the suffering they cause innocent civilians and animals alike."

After I hung up the receiver, I crossed the room to the kitchen window, staring at the lump under the blood-stained sheet beside my milkbox. What did it mean? More pressure from Tedesco to keep my big nose out of his business?

Or maybe …

I rushed into my bedroom, opened the closet door and reached into the pocket of my blue suit jacket to get that note Diane Black had given me at Robert's Restaurant.

I dialed the phone number and while I waited I studied the note: her handwriting was straight up and down, neat and precise, as you'd expect an accountant's to be – just four words: *If you need me*. Then the phone number. It was signed, *D.B.*

Did I need her? It pained me to admit it but, yes, I did.

Did she need me? Only if it suited her.

"Hello?"

"This is Max Dexter speaking, Mrs. Black. I want you to know that your scare tactics won't work with me."

"What scare tactics?"

"That dead dog left on my doorstep." My voice was quaking with anger. "You can't manipulate me. I won't play your game and neither will Frank Russo."

"Dead dog?"

"Please. Don't play dumb. That dog was dumped in exactly the same place as Bernie Fiore's body. Sometime after the police raid on the dog fights in the east end of the city."

A long pause on the line – then she finally said, "I'll look into this."

I was still holding the phone after she'd hung up and it felt like the dial tone was thumbing its nose at me. Was she really in the dark? Why would she have given me her number if it wasn't an offer of ... what?

I called for a cab to take me downtown. Dave was in the office so I asked to speak with him. "Another nasty shock on my doorstep this morning," I told him. "It was one of those fighting dogs, a dead and bloody mess." Then I related the news about the raid and subsequent arrests. "I'm sorry, Pal, if you get dragged into this too. We both have to be more careful now – these damn guys are capable of anything."

It took a long moment for him to answer in a shaky voice, "Okay, Max. I'm on my way."

Then I secured my revolver in its shoulder holster. As I did so I was reminded of a statement which some folks attributed to Al

Capone: "You can get much further with a kind word and a gun than you can with a kind word alone."

I decided to follow that advice.

CHAPTER TWENTY-THREE

IT WAS MID-MORNING BY THE time I reached my office and Iz rushed toward me as I entered.

"Thank goodness you're all right, Max. It's not like you to be this late without calling in. We were worried about you. I phoned several times but the line was always busy."

Phyllis took my coat and hung it up; then I sat down at the coffee table near the window where I poured some White Spot java. Both women sat beside me, one on either side, their eyes jittery as they awaited my explanation.

"I'm sorry I didn't call; I should have. I had a busy night and then I slept in." I told them about the tip-off from the newspaper carrier and the subsequent police raid on the dog fights and the arrests of some of those involved. I skipped the part about my nightmare; they didn't have to know every damn thing about me.

"When I went out to retrieve my milk this morning, I found another body dumped on my back porch."

Phyllis' eyes bugged out. Iz grabbed my hand and squeezed hard.

"It was a dead dog this time. One of those fighting dogs, bloody and mutilated. I covered it over and called Mr. Neatby to arrange for the SPCA to pick it up."

We sat in silence while my news filled the room with revulsion at the sickening image of that dead animal. And with a strong undertone of foreboding.

"It's obvious that I've got the attention of the gangsters who profit from these dog-fights and they're warning me off. But now I'm worried about the two of you – it's not likely, but it is possible, that you could become targets as a means of getting at me. So for the next few days, you should be on guard and take precautions;

be wary of anyone you don't know and try not to go anywhere alone. It's a good idea to take a cab to the office and back. And have the driver wait until you're safely inside."

Isabel's eyes were riveted on mine and I noticed the knuckles of her clenched fists were white. Phyllis sat on the edge of her chair, a hand to her mouth, her eyes blinking like she'd been awakened from a bad dream.

I got to my feet. "I know we can get through this. You're both strong women – and I'm grateful that you're by my side."

I entered my office and glanced at the mail but couldn't focus on it. I was feeling like a heel for bringing the menace of those mobsters into the lives of everyone around me, especially Iz and Phyllis. But I couldn't back off now. I felt a fiery compulsion in my core, urging me to join the battle against the Mob despite the threat to my hopes for a family life with Isabel.

I moved to my office window and stared at the brick wall next door where a grainy image of Diane Black slowly took shape. Behind her stood an army of mobsters, tommy guns aimed at me, awaiting her command to charge. She struggled to control a snarling pit-bull, straining against its leash. Then she dropped it and the beast hurtled through the window, teeth bared and drooling ...

A tap-tap on my office door shattered that vision and I turned to see Frank Russo striding into my office. "Jeez, Max, you sounded crummy on the phone but you look even worse in the flesh. Like someone scared the crap out of you."

"An overactive imagination," I said as I waved him in. Isabel had followed him and we sat around my desk.

"Those gangsters are giving him the shock treatment," she said to Frank. "One of those fighting dogs on his doorstep this morning. As dead as Bernie Fiore."

He swivelled in his seat. "Damn, that's a low blow. Guess you were right to suspect some kind of retaliation."

I nodded, wondering why he was here. "What's up, Frank?"

I watched his eyes flick to Isabel and back to me. "There's been a ... development."

"You can speak freely. Iz and I have no secrets."

He bobbed his head in her direction, then continued. "I just left the jail and thought I'd give you the news in person. Nick Fiore's in the hospital; he was knifed in the showers early this morning, blood all over the place. He's still alive – but barely, and was rushed over to the Hamilton General. But following jail-house etiquette, nobody else in the showers saw a damn thing.

"I had a talk with the Governor at the jail and he's guessing the knife artist was Bruno Spinelli. He's one of Tedesco's hard men who's awaiting transport to the Kingston Pen. He was convicted on a manslaughter charge –"

I grabbed his arm, interrupting him. "But what about Nick's chances? Is he going to make it?"

"No word yet. I won't be able to see him 'til this afternoon." He hunched forward in his chair. "And I'd like you to come with me. If Nick is responsive, you could tell him about your meeting with Bernie at the Tivoli. And his funeral. Then after you've softened him up, I'd like to squeeze him for details about that City Councillor's murder. So far, he's kept mum but we have to open that can of worms." Then he pointed an Uncle Sam finger at me. "And you could be the can-opener."

I glanced over at Iz; her lips were pursed as she stared at me, but she held her tongue.

Frank continued his spiel, "I hope to God he doesn't die before we get in to see him; he's my only witness and I need that bugger."

"All right, I'll go with you. Let me know when you're ready."

I stood up and we moved to the doorway.

"Oh, about that dead dog on your porch," he said as I opened the door, "look on the bright side. It means you've got those Mob guys on their toes. Keep up the good work, Pal."

We watched him clump across the outer office, shrug into his coat and tip his hat to Phyllis with a wolfish leer. "Be seeing you, Sister. Keep an on eye on that boss of yours."

Iz poked me in the ribs. "You two are a perfect match. A real pair of tough-talking sweethearts."

I grasped the finger she was using to jab me. "Not to change the subject, but how was that Accountants' Society wingding last night?"

"You should've been there. You'd have been the life of the party – and," she paused to straighten a lock of hair on my brow with her fingertips. "I just noticed that you've had a haircut, Max. It makes you look quite … debonair."

I lifted her hand away and held it. "Thanks. But you were saying about the party …?"

"Well, some of my former colleagues heard that I'd left my father's firm and they thought I was crazy to go into the detective business. After listening to you and Frank talk about Mob killings and dog-fights and stabbings in the jail, well, sometimes I wonder about it, too."

"It's not always like this, Iz. You know that. Most of the time we're just doing routine stuff: fact checking, interviewing people and gathering information for court proceedings. And some of that work can be downright boring."

She reached up to straighten my tie, then snugged it tighter at my collar. "I'm worried about you, Max. A dead man and a dead dog on your doorstep could mean you might be next." Then her arms wrapped around me, squeezing me tight against her breast. "I need you in my life," she whispered. "And I'm afraid I might lose you."

CHAPTER TWENTY-FOUR

I HAD SOME TIME BEFORE lunch so I decided to continue my search for Iz's Christmas present. Barely an inch of snow had fallen overnight and most of that had disappeared from the downtown sidewalks, which were again crammed with anxious shoppers. It made me wonder why some folks waited until the last minute to do their Christmas shopping. It was inconvenient for the rest of us.

My usual shortcut to James Street North was less busy and I limped across the street to Eaton's, recalling that diamond ring display I'd seen in their window. As soon as I'd gone through the revolving doors, I was swept forward on a tide of shoppers surging toward the bank of elevators at the rear of the store. At one point, I was face to face with a big bruiser who's accusing eyes bored into mine: I would've sworn it was Bernie Fiore but a few seconds later he, too, was pushed along by the crowd.

I managed to bail out at Tuxedo Rentals, where I caught my breath and slowed my breathing until Bernie's image faded away. It helped to watch the elevator operators for a moment. They were dressed in smart beige army-like uniforms, complete with cap, black low-heeled shoes, stockings with seams and white gloves. I admired their parade-square efficiency as they marshalled their patrons into their elevators to be delivered to each of the busy store's six floors. "Move to the rear of the car please and watch your step, Madam. Going up."

A life-sized cardboard Santa figure shouldering a bag of toys was displayed near the elevators: *Visit Santa in the Toy Department – 5th Floor*, and the times he'd be there were listed.

I managed to catch the eye of a manager walking toward me, carrying a clip-board, an Eaton's name-tag pinned to his jacket. I waved him down, "Pardon me, please. Which way to jewellery?"

He pointed to his right. "Two aisles over, near the silverware and clocks."

I was lucky. Just as I arrived, two women left the counter and I stepped in, catching a clerk's attention. She was short but well-built, with raven-black hair and skin as clear as porcelain. Her Eaton's tag read *Ann Muir.*

"I thought I'd get trampled to death," I said. "Is it always this busy?"

"This?" she shrugged. "This is nothing. You should see it the day before Christmas. It's a Chinese fire drill."

"Thanks, I'll be sure to miss it. Now, I'm wondering about the price of those diamond rings in the window."

She took her time inspecting me, top to bottom. When her eyes rested on mine she said, "You surprised me. I took you for a pearl kind of guy."

That caught me off guard. "Oh yeah? Why's that?"

When she looked up at me I noticed her eyes were as dark as her hair. "I'm not quite sure," she said. "It's kind of an intuition you develop after you're in this business for a while. But if you want a diamond ring, well, you're the customer and Mr. Eaton says you're always right."

She moved along the counter a few steps, bent down and removed a tray of rings just as the clerk at Birk's had done. "Here we are, a fine selection of engagement rings. They range in price from $129 to as much as you can afford to pay. What do you think?"

I looked over the glistening array. "They all look nice. But … I'm afraid they're a little out of my price range. What about diamond earrings? Maybe a nice diamond chip." I threw that in like an experienced diamond buyer.

She gave me a patient look and nodded. "Fine. I'll be right back."

I watched her scoot around the counter behind a glistening Christmas tree sprayed with blue sparkly snow. She returned with several small boxes and set them on the counter.

From the first box she removed a pair of earrings and displayed them on a black velvet pad. "These diamond chips are in a nice setting and they sell for $89." She removed one of her own earrings and replaced it with one of the diamond chips, then tilted her head back and forth.

Then she opened the next box. "Now, the setting is different on this pair. They're $69. Do you like them?"

I examined both pair as she modelled them. "No, that chip is just too small."

She opened the last box, removed a pearl earring and attached it to her ear. "This is what you really want. And they're only $49."

"Hmmm." I moved my head, looking at it from several angles. The box didn't say "Birks" on the lid and it wasn't blue but, what the hell, it was all I could afford. And they did look good on the saleswoman. "They certainly look more … substantial than those chips."

"Uh-huh. I thought you'd like them."

She returned the earring to its box and left it open while she closed the other two and set them aside.

"How'd you make me for a pearl kind of guy?"

An impish smile made a brief appearance. "Women's intuition, I suppose. You've got a bachelor sort of rumpled look about you – that suit and overcoat, they're okay, but off the rack, nothing fancy. But you seem like a nice fella. When I saw you coming to the jewellery counter you looked a bit lost and out of place. So I knew right away you were looking for something nice but not too expensive, for a certain someone. Then when you asked about the diamond rings I knew it was serious but those rings would probably be too much moolah for you. And you don't want a second-rate ring for a first-rate lady, right? But the pressure's on you; it's getting close to Christmas and you have to get her something, so you're thinking about diamond earrings as your second choice but the nice ones are out of your price range too. So I figure – pearls. The perfect compromise and maybe you'll wait for the diamond ring until you're up in the chips. How am I doing so far?"

"You'd better stop right there or you'll be telling me next what I had for breakfast this morning."

She gave me that tiny grin again. "Grape-Nuts by the look of that spot on your tie."

I paid the bill and wiped at my tie while she wrapped the pearl earrings in their tiny box with blue foil and a silver bow. Then I shook her hand and passed her my card. "Pleasure to meet you, Ann Muir. If you ever tire of this job, come and see me. I might be able to use another snoopy woman."

As I headed for the exit, I looked back over my shoulder. She was reading my card; then her head bobbed up and she was grinning at me.

CHAPTER TWENTY-FIVE

IT WAS LUNCHTIME WHEN I got back to my office. Phyllis was seated on the couch by the big window, eating a sandwich while she worked on her Barbara Ann scrap book.

"Isabel's gone to a Christmas lunch with her Loretto Academy friends. And I got you a sandwich from the White Spot. I left it on your desk, Max."

I thanked her, hung up my coat and entered my office where I stashed my present for Iz at the back of a desk drawer and ate my lunch.

Second thoughts about those earrings began to dance around in my head. Too small? Too impersonal? Pearls didn't carry the same commitment that diamonds implied but I just didn't have the dough for a diamond good enough for Isabel. And I had to accept the fact that I wasn't in the same league as she was – and probably never would be.

But what if Iz gives me something 10 times better? She might feel that I didn't reciprocate her feelings for me. Or, what if she just gives me one of those damn Christmas ties?

Shit – this was supposed to be a season of peace and goodwill – not some tit-for-tat businessman's bargaining ploy.

I stretched back almost prone in my chair, feet resting on the desktop as I stared at the ceiling, still puzzling about the suitability of those pearl earrings. A loud thump on my door startled me and I nearly catapulted over the desk when a voice with a Scots accent bellowed, "Max, my favourite nevue. Season's greetings."

I jerked upright in my chair and glowered at my Uncle Scotty. He was *The Spectator's* hot-shot crime reporter and was always badgering me for inside info I might have picked up from Frank Russo or elsewhere.

"Same to you, Unc, but I thought you didn't believe in Christmas."

"Wrong again, Laddie. Why, I've even brought you a little gift." From behind his back he produced a brown *Spectator* envelope imprinted, *Photo - Do Not Bend*, and laid it gently on my desk as though he were placing the baby Jesus back in his crib.

I stared at it a moment, then pushed the envelope back toward him. "Thanks but no thanks. I hate that photo."

"Now, now, don't be hasty. It's not what you think." Then he pulled up a chair and sat across from me. From his inside coat pocket he removed a mickey of Corby's Little Touch. From another pocket he produced two shot glasses and filled them to the brim, his veined drinker's nose twitching with anticipation.

"Bottoms up." In a swift and practiced motion he drained his glass and refilled it. "C'mon, my boy. 'Tis the season, after all."

I took a tiny sip and felt my eyes widen and my sphincter tighten. "Ouch, that'll get your attention."

"Just what I wanted. Now open that damn envelope."

I needed a souvenir 8x10 glossy of that *Spec* photo of me in my old clothes like I needed a night at the opera. But I opened it anyway. I slid it from the envelope and found myself gaping at an enlarged, grainy shot of Isabel and me looking across the table at Diane Black in Robert's Restaurant.

"Where the hell did you get this? It's an invasion of privacy."

He waggled his head. "You can't be private in a public place. Now, come clean. Why were you and your girl assistant meeting with a big-time mobster lady from the U.S. of A.?"

"How do you know we were? This woman in the photo could be Isabel's aunt or my landlady."

He reached for the Corby's and drained his glass. "No, no, no. Don't give me any of that malarkey. I've got a few pals on the police force so I know she's a player from the Miami Mob. But why in hell would she be meeting with you?"

I leaned back in my chair, breathing easier now because he hadn't recognized his sister-in-law. In fact, he'd probably never met her. When my father was killed and my mother skipped town, Scotty hadn't yet immigrated to Canada. It was years after my mother left Hamilton that Scotty had met and married her younger sister, Flo. When I'd eventually asked her, Flo claimed she knew nothing about my mother's whereabouts and, furthermore, she wasn't interested in finding out.

"I'm really sorry, Unc, but I can't tell you. I had to swear an oath of secrecy."

"Bullshit!" He slammed his fist on my desk and our glasses jiggled, spilling some of that panther piss onto my desk blotter.

I got up slowly from my desk, giving him my hard look. Then I crossed the room and held the door open.

He got to his feet, gulped down my drink and stuffed the mickey into his coat pocket, leaving the shot glasses behind. At the doorway, his face was alight in a crimson glow and his voice a coarse growl, "I'm disappointed in you."

"You forgot your shot glasses."

"They're not mine. They're Duffy's." Then he stomped out of my office, his anger trailing after him like muddy shoeprints.

CHAPTER TWENTY-SIX

I WAS SHUFFLING THROUGH THE day's mail, looking for something that wasn't a bill, when Frank Russo saved me with a phone call.

"I just heard from the Head Nurse on Nick Fiore's ward. She says I can see him this afternoon. How's 1400 for you?"

"It's good, Frank. I'll meet you in front of the *Spec*."

After he picked me up, Frank wheeled over to Barton Street past the jail and continued east the short distance to the Hamilton General Hospital, which occupied the large property between Wellington and Victoria Streets. Through the Barton Street entrance we stepped into the two-storey lobby which had become a scene from Santa's workshop. A towering Christmas tree was front and centre, aglow with coloured lights. Strung from the ceiling was a glittery banner proclaiming, *Peace on Earth*.

I pointed it out to Frank and he mumbled, "Not a helluva lot of that around here, is there?"

Beside a life-sized crèche scene, a choir of 30 or so school kids was doing its best with *"Adeste Fidelis"* while a semi-circle of old-timers, some in wheelchairs, were singing quietly along with them.

Frank crossed the lobby to the info desk while I waited in front of the elevators and hummed along with the choir.

"Third floor," Frank said when he returned, "unless you want to stay for the sing-along."

The nursing station upstairs was a hive of activity. And the queen bee was obviously the handsome woman in the nurse's uniform who stood at the counter, nose-to-nose with a tall young man wearing a white coat and a stethoscope necklace. Whatever they were arguing about had turned the doctor's face into a crimson oval as the nurse raised her voice. "Well, that's not how we do it here. Run along and have a word with the Chief Resident; he'll set you straight."

Frank paused a moment then stepped forward, holding up his badge. "Could we have a word, please?"

The young doctor turned and made his escape. I looked at the name-tag on the nurse's uniform – Claire Trépanier RN.

She shook Frank's hand and said, "I'm the Charge Nurse here. You're looking for Mr. Fiore?"

"That's right. I was notified that he's awake now and we could see him for a few minutes."

"Of course. But too bad, you just missed his doctor. And he's finished his rounds for the day."

"So what does the doc say?" Frank said. "Is he going to live?"

"He said it could go either way. Mr. Fiore's lost a lot of blood and he's still in critical condition." She took a step closer to Frank. "Now, I'm giving you five minutes tops. Then out you go."

Frank stood a little taller, sending her his cop's glare. "Now wait just a damn minute, Nurse. This is police business and we have our work to do."

She made an impatient waving motion with her hand. "Yes, yes. So get on your way and do it. Room 304 on your right, end of the hall. *Vite, vite.*"

We hustled along the corridor toward Nick's room. "What the hell's *veet, veet* mean? Any idea, Frank?"

"Not sure, but I didn't want to stick around to find out. I think it's French for get the hell outta here."

We arrived at 304, where an empty chair sat by the door. Frank was swiveling his head, looking up and down the hallway. "Supposed to be a goddamn guard on this door."

Then we heard the clump-clump of footsteps behind us, moving quickly our way. Frank spun around to face a uniformed cop.

"Shit, Hubbard, where the hell've you been? We need a guard on this room full-time. That means you don't wander around the halls, flirting with the nurses. This is important, goddammit – this prisoner could be in danger and we have to protect him. At least, until he talks."

The cop was shuffling his feet, waiting for his chance to speak. "Jeez, I was just takin' a leak, Sergeant. Gone two minutes –"

"Two minutes. That's all it takes to snuff the guy. Next time, tell the Charge Nurse or someone at the nursing station when you're away so they can keep an eye on this room and raise the alarm if something happens. Got that straight?"

"Ten-four, Sergeant. Won't happen again." He scuttled to his chair, plopped down and looked the other way.

We stepped into the room. It was much larger than I'd expected. Then I realized it was a double room with one of the beds removed. Nick lay on an elevated bed like a body on a hospital ship after Dieppe, his eyes clamped shut. His head was propped up on pillows and the tubes in his arm connected him to a couple of glass IV bottles dangling from a stand near his head. His mop of thick hair was the colour of anthracite against the Rinso-white pillows.

Memories of my long convalescence in England washed over me and it took me a long moment to shrug them away.

Frank opened the door to the washroom, went in and looked it over. I watched him rattle a connecting door, making sure it was locked.

We moved to Nick's bedside and Frank dipped his head down beside him. "Nick. It's Frank Russo. You okay to talk for a minute?"

He didn't respond and Frank touched his arm. "We won't stay long, Nick. You're in bad shape but we need to talk."

One eyelid lifted half-way, then the other. His lips were parched and when he moved them no sound came out. Frank picked up a glass of water from the side table and dabbed a few drops on Nick's lips with the end of a straw. Nick opened his mouth and Frank dabbed some more.

"School," he croaked. "Remember you from school."

"That's good, Nick. Max is here too. You remember he lived with my family on Hughson Street?"

He tried to lift his hand toward me but it must've felt like it was on fire because he winced and let it fall back on the bed. "Just a kid then ... Max."

"Yeah, I was. Not like you big guys, hangin' out at Pugliese's corner store, whistling at all the dames going by."

A ghost of a smile appeared on his parched lips and Frank put a few more drops of water on them.

"Frank and I were at Bernie's funeral. I guess you heard about his death on the jail's grapevine, eh?"

"More news than in the paper," his voice a weak whisper. "Most of it bad."

"It was a sombre ceremony," I said. "We saw your mother and father with the priest while he prayed over the casket."

Nick didn't try to nod but he blinked his eyes and I knew he understood how his parents must have suffered.

Frank was shuffling his feet, signaling me with his eyes to shut up and give him a chance so I backed away a step.

He lowered his head close to Nick. "I've got a couple of questions about you and Sal Angotti meeting that politician at Paddy Greene's. We know things got out of hand before the guy died. I asked you about this before but maybe you can remember now. Bernie said Sal popped him. Is that how it went down?"

For a few seconds I didn't think he'd cooperate. But I was certain that he realized he was knocking on death's door. And he had to know that Tedesco was responsible for his brother's death. We didn't have long to wait before he made up his mind.

He raised his eyes to focus on Frank. "Yeah. Sal was ... out of control. We were only supposed to scare the shit out of that guy so he'd vote the right way." He paused for a moment to lick his lips and take a deep breath. "Sal went nuts and sliced the bugger up. Knocked me out ... left me for the cops, the bastard."

He'd begun to pant and Frank reached for the water again.

But at that moment the nurse bustled into the room. "You've had your five minutes, Gents." She clapped her hands. "Chop, chop. Let's go."

Frank made a show of checking his watch and moved toward her. "Now look here, Nurse. We just got here and we need this man's testimony. It's an urgent police matter."

They stood there, nose to nose in a staring match – two big kids in the schoolyard, daring each other to throw the first punch. Nurse Trépanier snapped her left hand forward, clenching Frank's wrist and removed the glass of water with her right hand. She turned and set it on the side table. Then she gripped Frank's elbow, steering him toward the door. "This man's on the brink of death," she said, her voice lowered but Steel-City hard. "And he's not going to testify to anything if you don't allow him to recover."

She swiveled her head toward me, still at Nick's bedside. "You too, Mister. Time to skedaddle."

Back in the hallway, Frank was about to wind himself up again but the nurse moved to calm him. "Look here, we're sympathetic to the police. We know this is part of your job. But our patients' needs come first; you must understand that. Mr. Fiore is a strong man; the doctors think he has a 50-50 chance to recover, so back off for now and give him some time to recuperate."

I saw Frank's mouth beginning to open and I linked arms with him. "Let's go, Frank. Maybe we can see Nick tomorrow." And I tugged him in the direction of the elevators. As we were walking away, Frank turned back and shot a black look toward Hubbard, sitting up straight on his chair by the door and wearing what might've been a thin smile.

I tried to relieve the tension while the nurse was marching us toward the elevators. "You wouldn't be related to Robert Trépanier, would you? He works for Wentworth Security Services, here in town."

"'Fraid not," she said. "It's a fairly common French-Canadian name."

"Well, you speak English very well." Sometimes a compliment works wonders.

"No surprise there, Buster. I was born and raised in Welland."

I felt my face flush and I shut up. I was no match for this babe.

When the elevator arrived Frank passed her one of his cards. "My extension number's on there. Give me a call if there's any change in his condition."

She took the card but continued to look him in the eye, waiting.

Frank paused a long beat before he said, "Please."
A satisfied twitch of her lips, then she bustled away.

CHAPTER TWENTY-SEVEN

FRANK DROPPED ME OFF IN front of my building where pedestrians were moving along at a fast clip, heads bowed against a sudden squall of stinging snow pellets. In the elevator, Tiny said, "That uncle of yours has ridden upstairs twice to see you, Sarge. Reminds me of one of those yappy little dogs, running in circles, chasing its tail."

"If you see him again, tell him I'm on my Christmas vacation."

Tiny slid the door open on the third floor and I handed him a flat-fifty of Sweet Cap cigarettes with a red bow on it. "Merry Christmas, Pal."

A grin on his pixie face. "Thanks, Sarge. Same to you." And he shook my hand.

Phyllis wore a guilty look when I entered the office, a large clipping from the newspaper in one hand, a pair of scissors in the other.

"Oh, hello, Max. Please don't think that I work on my scrapbook all the time you're away from the office." She held up the clipping: *Police Raid Dog Fights in Hamilton East: Seven Local Men Arrested.* "I'm proud of you, Boss. It's too bad you don't get any credit in this story. After all, you were the one who found that location for the police."

I smiled at her. "Publicity's good for business most of the time, Phyl. But in this case, I don't want to be wearing a sign on my back saying, Attention Gangsters: This is the dope who sicced the cops on you."

Her eyes opened wider, "Ah, I see what you mean." Then she laid the clipping carefully aside.

"I appreciate your enthusiasm," I said. "But let's not make too big a deal about it."

I glanced over at Iz's empty desk. "Isabel have a meeting this afternoon?"

"No, something to do with her father. Here, she left you a note."

"Thanks." I checked my Bulova – almost 1600. "Why don't you pack up for the day? You could do some last-minute Christmas shopping if you're brave enough to fight the crowds."

"Oh, thanks, Max, you're such a good boss. I didn't want to ask for the time off but there's not much business here so close to Christmas."

After she left I sat at my desk and read Iz's note:

Dear Max,

My father's annual Christmas do is tonight and I feel obligated to be there. (Don't ask me why.) I knew you'd rather cut off your right arm than attend, so I didn't mention it. I have a few other chores before that, so I'll see you tomorrow.

Love, Isabel.

I breathed a sigh of relief, imagining her old man, J.B. O'Brien, doing his peacock strut among his rich pals and whispered, "Thank you, Iz."

Phyllis had left the remains of *The Spectator* on my table and I scanned it before closing up for the day.

I read that the latest Gallup poll showed 76% of Canadians preferred to have price controls re-imposed even though their taxes would rise. Nobody asked me about that.

And the Post Office announced there would be no regular mail on Christmas Day. However, special delivery service would be provided as usual. That might be the thin edge of the wedge, I thought. Next thing you know, they'll stop Saturday delivery.

The poor damn Brits were still under food rationing and I felt a bit guilty that we didn't have to put up with that anymore.

Syl Apps, captain of the Toronto Maple Leafs, was now raking in seven grand a year. I probably wasn't the only one who envied Syl Apps. Imagine, all that dough for chasing a little puck around a hockey rink. Hamilton steelworkers, who performed their dangerous work at Stelco, had bargained for a wage increase to forty-five smackers for a forty-hour week. So their annual pay was now $2,340. And lots of other workers earned less than that. It occurred to me again that "Something was rotten in the state of Denmark", as some writer-guy once said.

I folded the paper and tossed it into the waste basket. Then I glanced at my wristwatch again – almost 1700. Phyllis was right – there wasn't much business here when Christmas was just around the corner.

I locked up and crossed King Street to the cab stand in front of the Royal Connaught. I slid onto the front seat of the first taxi in line and I was astonished to see Lefty behind the wheel. "You remember how to drive? I thought you dispatchers never left the warmth of your cozy office."

He bellowed a laugh. "Not during Christmastime, Max. It's all hands on deck and the boss himself is on dispatch. Need a lift home?"

"Yep. Remember the address?"

"You betcha," He tapped his noggin with a knuckle. "Once it goes in, it's locked in forever. Corner of Emerald and Hunter, right?"

I entered my apartment, eased the door closed and remained still in the semi-darkness. Didn't smell any cigarette or cigar smoke and no aftershave or perfume, so I deduced I'd had no unwelcome visitors. Hung up my coat in the closet – no one hiding in there. Tip-toed through the kitchen to the rear door and peeked out – no dead bodies, canine or otherwise.

I had a quick supper: a cheese sandwich with a bowl of Campbell's tomato, washed down with a tall glass of Royal Oak. All the while I was thinking of Isabel at her father's soirée; the swells in their snug-fitting evening clothes, sipping their fancy French champers and sliding those slimy oysters down their gullets. I breathed another sigh of relief for Iz's non-invitation to that shindig.

I left the dishes in the sink and entered the living room where I put my feet up on the ottoman, leaned back in my comfy chair and picked up the newspaper. After a moment I realized I'd already skimmed it at the office. So I flipped to the back section for the radio listings.

I caught the tail end of the news on CKEY with Lorne Greene but heard nothing I hadn't already read in *The Spec*.

My favourite show, *The Thin Man*, wasn't on tonight so I tuned in WBEN, one of the Buffalo stations, and listened to *Mr. Keen, Tracer of Lost Persons*. He and his faithful assistant, Mike Clancy, tracked down missing people by using their superior powers of deduction. Much as Max and Iz did when they were on a case.

Mr. Keen was entering a darkened room and the creepy music was growing louder and creepier when the phone rang.

My phone.

I turned down the radio, went into the kitchen and picked up the receiver.

"Hello, is this Mr. Dexter?" A pleasant voice. Female.

"Yes, ma'am."

"This is Marilyn Edwards calling. You met my son, Trevor, the newspaper boy out by the airport."

"Of course. Is everything all right?"

"Yes, it's fine. And I'm sorry to call at this hour but I've been working evenings all this week. My boys were waiting up for me when I got home – all excited about that raid on the house with the dog-fights. And Trevor is so proud of helping you. I just wanted to thank you for treating him like a grown-up; he's at that age now where he doesn't want to be thought of as a child anymore."

"Well, he has every right to be proud, Mrs. Edwards. Without his tip-off the police wouldn't have arrested those men. Trevor's a smart young fellow and I'm sure his dad would have been proud of him. It's obvious you're teaching him well."

There was a pause on the line as I heard her catch her breath.

"Thanks for calling, Mrs. Edwards. I hope you and your boys have a Merry Christmas."

When I returned to the living room, I listened to my program for a few minutes but realized that Mr. Keen and his buddy were way ahead of me and I couldn't follow the story. So I snapped off the radio and decided to go to bed and read.

I puffed up the pillows and settled back in bed to read a new novel I'd picked up at the Hamilton Public Library: *I, the Jury* by Mickey Spillane. Maybe it was the picture of the sexy babe on its cover that attracted me. Or the blurb on the back that said Spillane was a Yank, a fighter pilot during the war, and he used to write comic books. Whatever the attraction, he seemed like my kind of guy.

I must've nodded off. My book had slid to the floor and the phone was jangling in the kitchen. I checked the wall clock when I got there – 2200.

"Max, it's Frank. You in bed already? The damn phone rang nine times."

"No, I was reading and I guess I dozed off. Where the hell are you? It sounds like a train station in the background."

"I'm at the General again. They called me about Nick –"

"Why? What's happened?"

"He's dead."

That snapped me awake. "Too bad, Frank, but you probably wouldn't have gotten him to testify anyway. Guess he died from loss of blood, eh?"

A long pause on the line.

"Frank?"

"Someone got into his room. Suffocated him with his pillow."

"Holy Hell. What happened to that guard on the door?"

"He'd disappeared."

"Wait a minute – it's hard to believe that anyone could've gotten past that Charge Nurse without her noticing."

"It happened right after the shift change, so she wasn't there. I talked with the night nurse who took over. She told me she'd spoken with a doctor she didn't recognize who'd picked up Nick's chart and gone in to see him. All quite normal, she said, and she thought no more about it. I asked about the cop on the door but she hadn't seen him there. Then she was called to an urgent case at the other end of the hall. Later, while she was making her rounds, she found Nick – dead in his bed."

"And where the hell was Hubbard?"

"We found him tied up and gagged in the closet. He didn't kick up a fuss because that so-called doctor had given him a good dose of ether."

"Jeez, this was well planned. Any idea who this 'doctor' was?"

"Well … he gave his name to the nurse …"

"C'mon, Frank. What's his damn name?"

"Dr. Dexter."

Shit in a mitt.

Why would the killer use my name? I suppose a watcher from the Mob could have been on duty and seen Frank and me earlier. Or maybe one of the orderlies was on their payroll. Whoever it was, we were seen going into Nick's room and spending some time with him. It wasn't Hubbard because he couldn't have tied himself up and gassed himself.

"It's gotta be Tedesco's doing," I said. "His guy at the jail muffed the job to get rid of Nick in the showers, so he had someone finish him off in the hospital. But why would he waste his time on Nick when the troops from Buffalo are breathing down his neck?"

"Beats the hell out of me, Max. Jeez, I'd be a nervous wreck if I was in his shoes. But maybe his brain is scrambled and he's not thinking straight – he's still got Max Dexter on his mind while his former pals are building the gallows."

"So what do you think I should do?"

"If I were you, I'd lie low and wait for the storm to blow over – I figure it won't be long now. But that ain't your way, is it?"

CHAPTER TWENTY-EIGHT

BACK IN BED, I HAD trouble getting to sleep again. Every time I started to snooze, one of Tedesco's guys would invade my dream and startle me awake as he tried to strangle me; later, another thug was giving me the pillow-over-the-face treatment like Nick Fiore.

I got out of bed for a drink of water. Twice. It didn't help. Just made me pee.

At 0200 I awoke in a sweat. My pajamas were soaked through so I had a bath and put on my other pair from the laundry basket. Then I fluffed my pillow and picked up my copy of *I, the Jury*, hoping it might put me back to sleep. But that didn't work either. I found myself getting mad at Mike Hammer: he was a brutally violent man and contemptuous of the law. Not my kind of guy after all. And he had no manners. So I put Mike to bed and snapped off the light, hoping for a couple hours of rest.

No such luck – this time I'd been dreaming that Tedesco himself was standing at the foot of my bed and one of his thugs had screwed the short barrel of his .38 into my right ear. I tried swatting the guy's hand away but he pressed even harder and I began shouting at him.

My eyes snapped open and I wished they'd hadn't.

That dream from hell wasn't a dream.

There was Tedesco, staring at me from the foot of my bed.

And one of his soldiers beside me; his revolver just inches from my head now and there was blood on the barrel. My right ear was pulsing with a fiery throb. When I touched it I got blood on my fingers.

Tedesco remained where he was and flicked a glance at his goon beside me. "Check the bedside table. See if his gun's there."

The guy pulled the drawer open and removed my .32 revolver from its holster, which he threw aside. He emptied the cartridges onto the floor and kicked them under the bed, then tossed the empty gun across the room near the closet.

Now he stood close beside me, his gun pointed at my head again.

Tedesco was giving me the evil eye as he cleared his throat. "I don't know what motivates you, Dexter, but you're like shit on a shoe – hard to scrape off and the stink lingers on."

I glared back at him, wishing I had one of those shitty shoes to bounce off his noggin. What was it he wanted from me? And how could I avoid it?

He moved around my bed, nudging his henchman aside as he got closer. "Wait outside, Sammy. And close the door."

When the guy had gone Tedesco bent over me, his breath as pungent as the garlic section in Nicastro's Grocery. "I need to see your mother alone. Without those visitors from Buffalo in the way. And *you* are going to arrange that meeting."

I stared up at him. He must be thinking he could sweet-talk Diane Black into some kind of arrangement that would leave him still in charge. Or at least alive so he could skip town and retire in peace. Fat bloody chance of that happening. And it was obvious he didn't know that I had zero influence with my mother.

"Listen," I said, trying to keep my voice from shaking, "until this week I hadn't seen the woman for 25 years. And she has no inclination to do a damn thing for me."

He leaned into me again, his black eyes flashing with menace. "Bullshit! You'd be a dead man now if it weren't for her."

My puzzled expression must have convinced him that I didn't know what he was talking about.

"Somebody told her about our little feud, you and me. And now the word's gone out that she wants her son protected – so it's hands off her precious little boy."

I gaped at him. How could I believe this guy? A Mob boss. Therefore a liar and a manipulator.

"I don't believe you. She wouldn't lift her little finger to protect me."

He leaned even closer; his face now inches from mine. "Listen up, Junior. You're going to get me in to see Diane Black. And she's going to arrange my safe passage out of Hamilton."

"You're dreaming. Why would she agree to that?"

His right hand shot forward and grabbed my throat, squeezing so hard I felt my eyes watering as I gasped for air.

"Because I've got your fancy girlfriend. I'm going to phone your office today at noon. If you haven't arranged a meeting with your mother and me by then, I'll kill Miss Isabel O'Brien."

He pushed me backward, banging my head against the headboard as he called out, "Sammy, get in here!"

Tedesco cocked his thumb in my direction. "Give this wise-ass one of my calling cards."

When I came to, I opened one eye – the other was stuck shut.

I saw the legs of my bed, dust balls on the floor. I reeked of vomit – my pajamas soaked through in a gooey mess. My head throbbed, my gut felt like a punching bag, and my bad knee was screaming.

Isabel.

I pushed myself to a sitting position and tried to get up but my leg crumpled and I crashed to the floor. I managed to crawl into the bathroom, pushing myself with the leg that still worked, cranked on the cold water, and stuck my head under the faucet, clenching my eyes shut as icy water streamed into my face and down the back of my neck. I turned off the tap and slumped beside the tub, catching my breath while I dripped all over the floor.

Isabel.

With Tedesco.

Goddammit.

I forced my eyes open when I heard the clinking of milk bottles. The early morning sun was streaming in my living room window; its rays piercing my eyes like red-hot needles. I didn't remember coming in here; maybe I'd crawled. Shivering, I looked down and saw I was in my underwear.

I tried to stand but collapsed back in my chair as though shoved by an invisible hand. Next time I got up by degrees, in slow motion. Much better. I felt my way into the bedroom to survey the carnage. That putrid odour still polluted the air; my dirty bed clothes reeked in a heap on the floor.

I got dressed in slow motion – it took 15 minutes for a two-minute job. Then I left all my mess where it lay and closed the bedroom door.

I made it to the kitchen but my stomach rebelled at the very thought of food. Feeling my way along the wall, I dragged my leg to the living room chair and collapsed.

Tedesco said he'd call at noon. When I bent my head to look at my watch a sharp pain shot up my spine and I gritted my teeth. It was 0930 and I ached all over. I was having a helluva time controlling the panicky thoughts galloping through my mind. Tedesco's exact words were, *"I've got your fancy girlfriend."* And those words kept bouncing around in my brain, repeating themselves like a broken record, taunting me.

Isabel.

At first I thought he might be bluffing. I believed he was in a panic because he was reading the writing on the wall, just as Frank and I had discussed. But I couldn't take the chance that he hadn't taken her. Nor could I depend upon Diane Black to finish her deadly business before something happened to Isabel.

Then my mind filled with an image of Iz, gagged and bound like Hubbard – that police guard in the hospital. Maybe she was hidden away in some filthy, abandoned warehouse in the city's east end – a couple of heavyweight thugs keeping watch and getting evil thoughts. A chill ran through me, head to toe.

I had to find her.

Now.

I groped my way back to the kitchen to use the phone and dragged a chair over beside it. I dialed Isabel's number and waited while my heart beat a tattoo in my chest. After 15 rings I hung up and tried again.

Same damn thing.

Then I called my office and Phyllis answered. "I've been worrying about you, Max. Here it is nearly 10 o'clock and both you and Isabel haven't appeared for work. Is anything wrong?"

"She didn't call to say she'd be late?"

"No, not a dickey bird. And I called her twice at home and got no answer. I sure hope she didn't have an accident or something."

Dammit. I wanted to believe that Tedesco was bluffing. But now ...

"I'm going to her place, Phyl. I'll call you later."

I hung up and dialed Iz's number again.

And again.

Then I called Frank at the cop shop only to learn it was his day off. I dialed his home number, gave him a quick report of Isabel's kidnapping and asked him to pick me up at my place.

"Fifteen minutes," he said. "And stay out of trouble until I get there."

CHAPTER TWENTY-NINE

I RETRIEVED MY REVOLVER FROM the bedroom where Tedesco's guy had tossed it across the room. I used the broom handle to swish the cartridges from under the bed and reloaded them. Then I found my holster in the corner beside the book case and strapped it on. I grabbed a full box of ammo from the top shelf of the closet, wincing from a renewed wave of pain as I reached for it, then stuck it in the pocket of my overcoat in the front hall.

When Frank arrived I opened the door before he could knock. "What took you so long?"

He grabbed my arm and steered me toward the living room. "Slow down for God's sake. Let's take a minute to figure out what to do."

Easing me onto the sofa he sat beside me. "My god, you look awful." He hustled into the kitchen and brought me some ice in a dishcloth. "Here. Hold this over that eye, and tell me again what happened – nice and slow."

I took a deep breath and repeated my story. "And if I don't arrange a meeting with Tedesco and my mother by noon he says he'll … kill Isabel."

"You're under your mother's protection? No damn wonder Tedesco's got his ass in a knot about Max Dexter. And it's a clever move on his part to use Isabel as his ticket out of town."

I couldn't sit there a second longer. "C'mon. Let's get going. We'll start at her place."

On our way to the door, Frank stuck his head into my bedroom and quickly slammed it closed. "Whew. Stinks to high heaven in there."

We were driving fast along Hunter Street toward James South and Frank said, "Remember Sal Angotti? Nick said he knifed that City Controller at Paddy Greene's?"

"Yeah."

"They fished him out of the canal this morning – a couple of holes in his skull. So the gang war's officially underway. They're cleaning house and I'm wondering why Tedesco is still pissing around, trying to make a deal. If I were in his shoes, I'd be on one of those big new airliners to South America."

I glanced over at him as he wheeled through a left turn onto James Street. His jaw was clenched, a dark scowl distorting his features. "Not a helluva lot we can do when these shoot-outs get underway," he said. "Makes you feel like an undertaker – following the Mob around and hauling the bodies away. Dammit, I should be getting a commission from Dermody's Funeral Home."

Frank turned right onto Aberdeen. Iz's home was on Ravenscliffe, a couple blocks down on the left. After he made the turn, he slowed the car and ducked his head to gawk at the big homes here. I pointed to her driveway and he pulled in and parked. He stood beside the car and stared up at the house. "What did you call this, a carriage house? Shee-it, Max. You told me Isabel's family was well off, but this is rolling in dough. I had no idea. She doesn't go around with her nose in the air so ... jeez, I just didn't know."

"C'mon, Frank. Let's go, we're wasting time."

I brushed away the light snow from the small windows in the garage door with my glove and looked in. Her car was still there. I'd advised Iz and Phyllis to take cabs for a couple of days which might explain why she didn't drive herself today. Frank called over from the front door. "It's locked and doesn't look tampered with."

The driveway and sidewalks were cleared and it hadn't snowed overnight, so they were no fresh footprints to follow out here. We walked to the rear of the house; no shoe prints anywhere in the thin layer of snow on the patio or the backyard. I tried the doors, also locked, no sign of forced entry. No broken windows.

"Tighter than a drum. I don't like it, Frank, she usually drives to the office but her car's still in the garage. She might've taken a cab but she didn't get there and she didn't call in."

I didn't have a key to her house and I didn't want to break in. I could call her father but I'd have to listen to another tiresome rant about how I was ruining his daughter's life and to hell with that. "You used to have a little set of tools, Frank. Still got them?"

He shot me a black look. "I don't use them much. Only in a dire emergency."

"Well?"

"I'll get them from the car."

We were on the patio again, Frank down on one knee, jiggling the little brass picks in the door lock. He had it open in less than a minute.

We stepped inside, took off our shoes and set them by the door.

I pointed to the staircase. "You check upstairs. I'll do this floor."

The dining room was undisturbed and I followed the scent of Christmas into the living room where a tall decorated tree occupied the corner near the picture window. Against the opposite wall was an immense fireplace, almost big enough to stand in. A row of Christmas cards marched along the stone mantle. No sign of a disturbance in here.

The kitchen showed signs that she'd been interrupted at breakfast. A cereal bowl, a small plate and some cutlery were on the table beside her half-full coffee cup. The bastards had been bluffing. They hadn't taken Iz until after they'd worked me over.

Iz's bedroom was on the main floor at the rear of the house, overlooking the garden. I drew back the drapes – a large window that didn't open was flanked by two smaller ones, both of which were locked. The only similarity between this bedroom and mine was the name. An acre of bed faced the windows onto the rear garden where the flowerbeds were outlined in snow and tall maples waved their leafless branches.

Two chests of drawers and an antique wardrobe occupied the wall nearest me. On another wall she'd hung a gallery of pictures;

some were photos of people and places I didn't know, others were landscape paintings – one of which was by our friend, Roger Bruce, from a recent exhibition at the Art Gallery of Hamilton.

I saw an open jewellery box on her dressing table and leaned down to have a look. Bracelets and necklaces along one side of the large box, rings and jewelled pins on the other. In the cen- tre was a selection of earrings and I sat on the bench for a closer look. Most of them sparkled with diamonds and other stones. I picked up the single pair of pearl earrings to examine them – they were much larger than the pair I'd bought at Eaton's and twice as brilliant.

Dammit.

There were doors at each end of the long wall behind the bed. Carefully replacing the earrings where I'd found them, I opened the nearer door and flicked on a light switch. A bank of ceil- ing lights illuminated the long, narrow space and I could've been in Eaton's Ladies Department; Isabel's clothing hung on racks which ran all the way to the door at the other end. It was the biggest closet I'd ever seen. On the end wall was a floor to ceil- ing mirror that reflected the image of a guy spending more time than necessary snooping around a woman's boudoir.

Yet another door led to a bathroom, also of a scale to match the rest of her home. By now I was feeling like a peeping Tom. This was a massive invasion of Isabel's privacy, but I persuaded myself that I had no choice. Nothing seemed out of place in the bathroom, so I closed the bedroom door, went to the front hall and called to Frank, "All clear up there?"

He appeared at the top of the stairs. "Three bedrooms and an office full of accounting books, typewriter and a couple other machines on the big desk. But nothing out of the ordinary. Well, I mean, not out of the ordinary for a palace like this. Jeez, she's got two bathrooms up here. Now I know how the other half lives," he said. "And I'm jealous as hell."

I slumped on the bottom step of the stairs as a wave of nausea threatened to overtake me.

I ached from head to foot.

Frank hurried down and sat beside me. "You sure you're okay, Max? You should be home in bed – I'll let you know the minute we find Isabel."

"Give me another minute. I can't stop now."

Frank's arm was around my waist as we made our way to the door at the end of a long hallway which led to the basement. He stopped and gawked out a tall, narrow window at the end of the hall toward the sprawling backyard of the large estate beside Iz's home. He turned to me, wearing his big-brother face. "Isabel's a mile out of our league, Bud. Hell, a hundred miles. You sure she's serious about *you*?"

His question didn't surprise me – Frank and I had skirted this subject before. I think he believed that Iz was a temporary fascination on my part and sooner or later I'd come to my senses. "I know why you're asking, Frank. God knows, I've asked myself the same question a thousand times."

"And what's the answer?"

"No time for that now. C'mon, we've got to find her."

Going down the basement stairs, my knee screamed with every step and I clutched the handrail as I gritted my teeth. I had to sit down on the bottom step while Frank looked around.

"Separate rooms for the heating system and water tanks," he called out as though he were taking inventory down here. "Two big storage rooms full of boxes and garden furniture. Along the end wall here, there's a workbench and gardening tools all in neat order."

Frank returned to the stairway and slumped down beside me. "This house has got everything but Isabel. And not a damn thing to tell us where she might be."

He looked as frustrated as I felt. "Any bright ideas, Frank? You're the police sergeant."

"Nope. But you're the private dick – supposed to be smarter than us dumb cops."

When I didn't respond right away, he said, "What? You think of something?"

"Well, maybe …"

"Tell me."

"This might sound crazy, but I'm thinking about calling my mother. If anyone can get info out of the Mob, it'll be her."

Frank was quiet for a moment while he chewed on that. "You'd do a deal with the devil?"

"Damn right. If it meant getting Isabel back."

He pushed himself up and pulled me to my feet. "Okay. It's worth a try."

He helped me upstairs where I picked up the phone in the kitchen. "I'm calling my office first, to see if there's any news."

I spoke with Phyllis. No news.

I dug out the note with the phone number on it and dialed Diane Black for the second time.

It rang three times while I held my breath and swallowed my pride. When she picked up I said, "It's Max calling. And I need your help."

Silence on the line. I could feel the sweat forming in my armpits. The receiver became slippery in my hand.

"It must be a matter of life or death," she said.

"It is. Isabel's been kidnapped by Tedesco. He broke into my apartment during the night and told me he'd release her in exchange for a meeting with you – without your friends from Buffalo present. If you refuse to see him, he says he'll kill her." I paused. "Please … Diane. I need your help."

The line went silent again for a few seconds, but it felt like an eternity.

"Give me the number you're calling from."

I gave her the number.

"Stay where you are. I'll call you back."

When I attempted to thank her, she stopped me and said, "Believe me, I know what it cost you to call me."

Then she hung up.

I was staring out the kitchen window, seeing Isabel's eyes in my mind, wide with terror.

I felt so goddamn helpless. Useless.

I replaced the receiver and wiped my hand along my pant leg before turning to Frank.

"So, what did she say?"

"She'll call back."

We sat at the kitchen table while we waited. Frank was drumming his fingers, staring out the window.

"Thanks for your help, Frank. I know it's your day off and you're busy at home with Christmas almost here."

He turned back to me. "Finding Isabel is more important. There'll always be another Christmas."

Minutes later the phone rang and I snatched up the receiver, almost dropping it. "Hello? ... hello?"

"Here's the address, Max."

She gave me a number on Caroline Street North and I had to grip the pencil hard to keep my hand from shaking. "I'm ... I'm grateful for this ..."

"I haven't earned your gratitude. I know I'm a failure as a mother but I chose the life I'm living ... and I can't turn back now. ... Good luck to you and Isabel."

My mind was spinning out of control. I felt like one of those fight dogs in training, racing on a merry-go-round, unable to stop. But I was relieved that I knew where Iz was being held, hopeful that she was still alive, and surprised as hell that my mother had helped me when I most needed it.

"Thank you ... Mother," I said, and hung up the phone.

CHAPTER THIRTY

FRANK SLOWED THE CAR AFTER he turned right on Caroline Street, heading toward the bay. Many of the homes here in the North End had been converted to rooming houses during the Depression when a lot of families took in boarders to make ends meet; then the war came along and things got even worse. As we neared the train yards which skirted the west end of Hamilton Harbour, the houses became more run-down, some of them abandoned and boarded up.

At the corner of Barton Street, we idled beside a vacant lot, now used as a makeshift dump; it was piled high with rusted-out car bodies, tires, and bed springs – all sorts of detritus. Beside it, the living room of a two-storey frame house had been converted into a small grocery/confectionery store. It looked like it was still open; a car was parked out front and I saw a man leave, pocketing a pack of cigarettes. A hand-lettered sign in the window said, *No Credit*.

Across Barton Street on the bay side, only a few houses remained standing. The area was apparently being cleared for some industrial purpose – two bulldozers were parked near the roadway but there was no activity here today. Frank drove on until we stopped in front of the address which my mother had given me. We stood on the gravel driveway and looked around, buffeted by a north wind howling off the bay. Plenty of truck traffic steamed up and down Barton Street. And freight cars were shunting back and forth on the maze of tracks in the marshalling yards beside us.

The house appeared to be unoccupied, no curtains on the windows, so we mounted the rickety steps. Frank peered through the small window in the front door. "Looks empty," he said.

Two mailboxes were screwed to the wall beside the door jamb, no names on them and I found them both empty. Frank carefully tried the door but it was locked.

"Wait for me here," he said. "I'll go around the house, and see if there's another way in. Some of these old places have a basement door." Then he unbuttoned his coat and withdrew his revolver which was holstered on his left hip. "I hope you remembered to bring your hardware."

I got my gun out. "Make it snappy, Frank. We don't have time to waste."

He was back in less than a minute. "Basement door in the rear – no lock, just a latch but I didn't go in – if anyone's down there, I didn't want to spoil the surprise."

He removed his magic tools from his pocket and had the door open in less time than it took him at Isabel's place.

We stepped in quickly and he closed the door. Dark and gloomy in the hallway, a musty odour in the air. To our left was a solid door with a sign on the wall beside it, *Apt. 1*. A long hallway led to a partially opened door toward the rear of the house. A staircase on our right, an arrow pointing upward with *Apt. 2* stenciled on it.

I tried the door to the apartment beside me; it was open. "I'll take this way," I said. "You go in the door down the hall and we'll meet in the middle."

The door creaked as I entered. The room was empty, and the smell of dust and decay hung in the air as though the house itself had died. When I closed the door I noticed a 1940 calendar from a Supertest gas station was pinned to it. The top section displayed a picture of the Dionne quintuplets standing in a row behind five birthday cakes. One of the quints was blowing out her sister's candles.

I passed through a small dining room, also empty, then into a barren kitchen where Frank was looking out a rear-facing window. "Not a stick of furniture," I said. "How about you?"

He turned to face me, pointing to an open door, "I checked the bedroom in there – nothing if you don't count the three wire hangers in the closet. Bathroom's got a sink, tub and a toilet – all filthy – the water's been shut off. Along the hallway there's a door to the basement but let's leave that 'til later and look upstairs now."

I followed him up the stairs which creaked and complained like my throbbing knee, courtesy of Tedesco's goon.

Upstairs, we found the same layout as the first floor apartment – I turned left toward the living room and Frank went ahead to the kitchen.

The entrance door felt blocked when I tried to open it. I pushed harder and heard something slide away from the door – and a terrifying image of Isabel's broken and mutilated body took hold of me until I got it open wide enough to squeeze in. It took a long moment for my heartbeat to slow as I scanned the room.

No Isabel.

It was a smelly mattress that blocked the door; in its centre were ancient urine and blood stains. But at waist height along the wall in the living room, I noticed what looked like faint streaks of dried blood so I followed that trail through the empty dining room then into the bedroom. Frank was already there, standing beside a narrow iron cot near the closet.

I rushed toward him, "Find something, Frank?"

"She isn't here." He pointed to some blood spatter on the wall. "But she might've been."

I touched the splotch with my fingertip. "It's not quite dry. I saw some smudges in the other room, too. If it's her blood, they must've taken her somewhere else."

The cot was a jumble; no sheets on the dirty mattress but a stinky brown blanket lay balled up on the floor. A bedside table had been overturned, the lamp smashed into pieces beside it. I knelt on my good knee and peeked under the cot – layers of dust and dirt. But my nose wrinkled as I caught the faintest wisp of Isabel's perfume.

If I hadn't checked down here, I wouldn't have noticed the crude design on the frame of the cot. "Take a look here, Frank."

He leaned down and I pointed to where the blood was smeared. "Looks like someone tried to draw an arrow with their fingertip or something blunt. It's pointing down. So she might be in the basement."

He gave me a bleak look, his eyes grave when he gripped my arm to help me up. "Or ... was."

CHAPTER THIRTY-ONE

BACK DOWNSTAIRS I RUSHED FOR the door to the basement, but Frank grabbed my coat and hauled me back. "Hang on, Max. If she's down there, she might have company. If so, they must've heard us tromping around up here so they could be waiting for us to leave. So here's what we're going do – I want you to go behind the house to that basement door an 1 I'll use the stairway in here. On a 10-count, no – better make that a 20-count to allow for your limp – we'll go in together."

I went out the front door and followed the narrow walkway around the house, counting – 11, 12, 13 ... there was still a light covering of snow back here and I slowed my pace as I rounded the back corner so I wouldn't fall ass over tea kettle. I was in position on the count of 18, then paused two beats and I was through the basement door and moving along a darkened hallway in a crouch toward the centre staircase.

I froze in my tracks when I heard the ear-piercing crack-crack of two gunshots and a muffled groan; then the unmistakable thud of a body tumbling down the stairs. I flattened myself against the wall, making an effort to slow my breathing. There was no more shooting so I eased myself forward until I reached the staircase. A body lay crumpled on the bottom steps, his head on the basement floor – unconscious or ...

It was Frank.

At that moment another gunman stepped from a doorway down the hall and came running toward me, his arm extended, his gun pointing straight at me. I tried to flatten myself against the wall and a bullet whistled past my right ear. I got off two shots and the guy crashed to the floor face-down, his gun skidding along the hallway in my direction. He didn't move.

I eased myself to the floor beside the stairs, out of the line of fire from above. Frank's head was turned toward me, eyes closed, breathing through his mouth in raspy gulps. I saw a bloody goose egg developing on his skull and more blood oozed onto the floor from somewhere near his mid-section.

I took a quick peek around the corner of the wall, looking for the shooter upstairs. A big guy wearing a Hamilton Tigers team jacket stood partway down the stairway. I couldn't see the guy's head and shoulders from this angle so he couldn't see me. But I sure as hell saw the big Army .45 he was levelling at Frank to shoot him again. I raised my revolver and put two slugs into his chest. His body reared back, his head slamming against the stairs and he slid feet-first, almost on top of Frank.

How the hell did we miss spotting this guy when we searched upstairs? I remembered checking the first-floor door to the basement and seeing no-one down here. But looking up the stairs now I could see the landing was wide enough to conceal someone in the shadows beside the door.

I remained where I was, controlling my breathing while I waited, in case another gangster appeared. A minute later, I'd heard nothing further and turned my attention back to Frank. For starters, I yanked the dead guy a few feet away from him. Then I checked on his partner down the hall – his gangster days were over, too.

Taking care, almost in slow motion, I turned Frank onto his back on the hallway floor. I opened his coat and suit jacket, looking for where he was shot. Blood seeped from a wound high up on his left thigh. I cut away his pants with my pocket knife to reveal a long bloody groove where a bullet had plowed along his upper leg toward his hip. Frank always wore a clean handkerchief in his suit jacket pocket so I used that to wipe around his wound then placed it on top. I couldn't tell where the bullet might have lodged, but I had to stop the bleeding.

I'd put on a clean white shirt this morning so I peeled off my coat and suit jacket and removed my shirt as quickly as I could, then I tore it into wide strips and bound up his wound. I moved over to the dead guy and cut off his pant legs with my knife. I ripped them into long pieces and wrapped them tightly over what used to be my shirt to put pressure on the wound and slow the bleeding. Then I put on my jacket and coat.

Next, I grabbed Frank by the ankles and tugged him slowly back toward the stairs. He slid easily along the floor, lubricated by his own blood. I parked his feet on the step above the level of his heart. I pulled the overcoat off the guy down the hall and covered Frank with it. He seemed to be breathing a bit easier now and I hoped he hadn't also suffered a concussion or worse when he whacked his head as he bounced down the stairs.

Now I had to find Isabel.

I pocketed Frank's revolver and picked up the hoodlum's .45 from the floor and stuck it my other pocket. I kicked the second guy's gun along the floor toward him where it lodged under his body and I left it there.

I continued along the hallway to the room from which that gangster had appeared and I peeked in. A single light bulb dangled from the ceiling but in its dim glow I noticed a long bundle on the floor beside the wall. It appeared to be wrapped in a blanket like a mummy and my heart skipped.

I moved slowly toward it, gun extended, and stared down at the terrified face of Isabel O'Brien, her panicking eyes wide and jittery, her mouth plastered with a wide band of surgical tape. Maybe she'd been wrapped for transport elsewhere and we'd arrived just in time.

I replaced my gun in its holster, knelt on one knee beside her, held her face in my hands and kissed her on the forehead. Then I carefully removed the tape from her mouth. Her breath came panting out in short gasps like a marathon swimmer.

"I'm okay, Max, and I'm so relieved you are too. I heard all those shots out there. What happened to those men? Are you alone?"

I placed my forefinger against her lips to quiet her. "Listen to me. Iz."

She struggled to free herself but slumped against my arm. "Oh, Max –"

"We don't have time to talk now. Frank was shot and he's unconscious in the hallway. Two gangsters were gunning for me out there and I had to shoot them. Did you see any others?"

Her head turned toward the doorway as though she expected another mobster to barge into the room.

I grasped her shoulders and squeezed. "Iz, look at me." I raised my voice. "Were there more than two men?"

She shook her head and winced. "I don't know for sure. But I only saw two of them."

"Are you hurt?" I ran my fingers lightly through her hair and felt a sizeable bump developing at the back of her skull and there was blood on my hand when I removed it. "Did they hit you on the head with something?"

"They weren't gentle when they threw me to the floor upstairs. And down here, my head hit that stone wall when they dumped me and I must've passed out. I'm still a bit dizzy. Is Frank all right? Tell me what happened."

"I'm going to set you free, Iz. Then I need to call an ambulance for Frank. He's lost a lot of blood."

The heavy blanket wrapped around her was secured by wide strips of packing tape at her ankles, waist and chest. I cut the tape with my pocket knife and peeled away the blanket. Her skirt had ridden up around her waist and I tugged it down.

She gulped several deep breaths, then slowly moved her stiffened limbs. "That feels better already, Max." Her voice croaked when she spoke.

"Don't try to get up." I moved forward and helped her scoot on her rear end a couple of feet back toward the wall where I propped her up and placed the blanket over her legs. "I'm going to phone for an ambulance from the corner store. Here, I'm giving you my gun in case another one of those gangsters shows up. If you have to use it, fire just as I showed you at the gun club. Remember to hold it in both hands, aim for his middle and squeeze the trigger, don't yank it. I know you can do this if you have to, Iz. I'm depending on you. And so is Frank."

I reloaded my revolver and placed it in her hands, aiming the barrel down, and I backed away from her. "I'll be back in a couple of minutes. I promise."

I hurried out the basement door and stopped at the corner of the house. Frank's was the only car out front, no sign of more unwanted visitors. It made me wonder how those two gunmen got here. I hadn't seen another car.

In my haste I'd forgotten to get Frank's car keys but I didn't go back for them; I could probably cover the half a block to the corner faster than if I went back for the keys and drove there. So I limped in double time to that little store on the corner of Barton Street, my battered knee complaining with every step I took.

An old man leaned against the counter, smoking a cheroot while he leafed through a newspaper. His head jerked up when I barged through the door and slammed it shut with my foot. I was leaning over, my hands on my knees, panting and trying to catch my breath. By now, my bum knee felt ready to explode, my eye and ear throbbed, and I clenched my jaw to keep from screaming.

After a moment, I was able to speak. "I need to use your phone. It's an emergency."

He shook his head from side to side. *"No inglese."*

My Italian was worse than rusty; I hadn't used it for years. I'd picked it up when I lived with Frank's family, but I'd forgotten much of it since then. I pointed to the phone on the wall behind him. *"Telefono, per favore."*

He frowned and proceeded to give me hell in rapid-fire Italian. I didn't catch what he said and I didn't have time to argue. So I yanked out my wallet, leaned across the counter and flashed it quickly open and closed in his face. *"Polizia,"* I said.

He spun around, grabbed the receiver and stuck it in my hand. The phone cord was taut so I remained half-sprawled over the counter in order to use it. I got the operator and asked her to connect me with the police. After a bit of rigamarole at the cop shop, I finally reached Frank's boss, Staff Sergeant Lantz. "Officer down," I told him. "It's Max Dexter calling. Frank Russo's been shot and needs an ambulance. And you can send the coroner's van for a couple of Tedesco's boys."

I gave him the location of the building and told him to hurry, that Frank needed a medic right away. Then I passed the phone back to the old guy. *"Grazie,"* I said and I hurried out the door.

Back at the house, I slumped against the basement wall for a moment, catching my breath and resting my throbbing knee. Then I withdrew Frank's gun from my coat pocket and entered the shadowy hallway, moving slowly along the wall in a crouch to check on him. The metallic tang of human blood was almost overwhelming down here and my stomach began to churn.

I got down beside Frank; he was still unconscious and his breathing remained laboured but that big bandage on his wound didn't look much bloodier than before. I moved to the dead gangsters – they were still dead. But I noticed a trail of blood stains on the floor where the big guy in the Tigers jacket had been dragged a few feet beyond where I'd left him.

Shit.

What the hell did that mean?

Isabel wouldn't have moved him: therefore someone else had arrived in my absence. I hadn't seen another car out front but it might've been stashed on the far side of the house, tucked out of sight, maybe where the dead gangsters had parked.

I got to my feet and didn't move a muscle, listening for the visitor. Not a sound other than Frank's heavy breathing. Then I tiptoed along the hallway to the room where I'd left Iz and poked my nose around the corner.

She sat in the same position where I'd left her, leaning against the wall, gripping my gun in both her hands, aiming it squarely at me. "It's Max, Iz. Don't shoot."

I stepped forward after she lowered my revolver.

A young guy in a black overcoat lay crumpled on the floor in front of her, his black fedora upside down on the floor near his head, his gun clutched in his right hand. His eyes were open wide and he seemed to be staring at Iz, not believing she'd shoot him.

I rushed toward her and grasped her right wrist, then pried my revolver from her ice-cold grip.

"I had no choice," she said in a hoarse whisper, her eyes riveted on the corpse at her feet. "He said he was going to ... kill me."

I got down beside her and wrapped her in my arms, squeezing her tight against my chest. I whispered in her ear, "Just hold on to me. I love you, Iz."

We huddled there on the floor, clutching one another and shivering as the tension began to ebb away.

The shrill wail of police sirens pulled us apart. "Cavalry's riding to the rescue," I said. "But I want you to stay here – I'm worried about that big bump on your head. The medics can take a look at it, just to be sure."

"But, Max –"

"Just humour me. Please."

She made a shooing motion with her hand and I eased her back against the wall.

CHAPTER THIRTY-TWO

I STOOD BESIDE THE DRIVEWAY and watched the cops arrive like an invading army, sirens blaring and lights flashing. Three police cars bounced along the roadway; two of them parked on the shoulder; the third drove in and parked behind Frank's car. Staff Sergeant Lantz got out and waved me over. "Which floor are they on?"

"In the basement. There's a rear door that'll be easier for the ambulance guys. Frank's in the hallway at the bottom of the stairs. He's unconscious and there's still some bleeding. There's also a pair of Tedesco's guys nearby – both of them down for the count. Another body in a room down the hall where they were holding my assistant. She's safe now but she had to shoot a new arrival while I was at the corner store phoning for help. She's got a big bump on her head and I think she should go with Frank to the hospital to have it checked."

He stepped toward me and gripped my shoulder. "Good man. Stay with me and we'll talk more in a minute."

Then he waved to one of the cops out on the road. "Hey, Mike. It'll be quicker if you have the ambulance guys come in along the side of the house so they can use the basement door. The ground's almost frozen so they shouldn't have any trouble."

He signaled to the cops in the other car and they jumped out and hustled toward us. "I'm going in the back door with Dexter here –" He turned back to me. "Front door locked?"

"Not anymore," I said. "The first and second floors were clear when I went to the corner to call you. I was only gone five minutes, but it wouldn't hurt to check."

"Okay. Gibbens, you and Mike go in the front door. A quick look around upstairs, then meet us in the basement." He turned to the other guy, a young constable, "You're with me, Springer. Let's go."

The rookie cop hesitated, then pointed at me. "But this guy's just a civilian, Boss – he'd only get in the way."

Lantz took a quick step toward him so they stood nose to nose and he pointed at me. "This guy was a military policeman who saw action overseas and he was a Mountie before that. So keep your lip buttoned and your eyes open. Maybe you'll learn a thing or two."

Downstairs, I showed the cops the scene and explained that Frank and I had been searching for Isabel. "I saw two Mob guys – the one who shot Frank was waiting in ambush on the landing up there. Frank tumbled down the stairs and I was able to clip the shooter. The other guy came out of the room where Isabel was tied up. He missed with his first shot and I didn't.

"I freed Isabel then hurried to the corner where I called you. While I was gone another guy showed up and was about to attack her. I'd left her with my revolver and she shot him."

Two of the ambulance attendants rushed along the hallway toward us, carrying a stretcher. The Detective Sergeant directed them to Frank. "Take Sergeant Russo first." He pointed to me. "This man gave him first aid and he can tell you what he did. And there's a woman down the hall who might need treatment."

They loaded Frank onto the stretcher and carried him out the back door to the ambulance. I went with them and explained how I wrapped his wound and tried to slow the bleeding.

One of the attendants remained with Frank and I accompanied the other to examine Isabel. Lantz was on one knee speaking with her in the room down the hall and he stood when we entered.

"This is one brave woman, Dexter. I hope you realize how lucky you are."

Iz piped up, "He's learning."

The medic knelt beside her. "Let's have a look at that bump."

She leaned forward and he examined the back of her head. "Quite a bit of blood from this scrape along your scalp – you'll probably need some stitches. Have you been dizzy? Nauseous?"

She shook her head and I saw her wince. "Well, maybe a little."

The guy stood up and brushed off his knees. "Might be a concussion. It's best to have it checked at the hospital."

I wanted to go to St. Joe's with the ambulance but there wasn't room and I hated to see it leave without me. Frank's boss offered to drive me after he'd deployed his troops. He pointed to the cop he'd called Mike. "You and Gibbens wait here for the coroner's people to pick up the bodies, then get back to the station to write up your report. I'll meet you back there."

He turned to the rookie and said, "Heads up, Springer," and tossed him a set of keys on a ring. "Drive Sergeant Russo's car to the station and wait for me there."

CHAPTER THIRTY-THREE

I SLID ONTO THE FRONT seat of Lantz's car and when he stopped at the corner of Barton Street I pointed out the little store I'd called him from. He nodded toward a black Plymouth parked beside it – a couple of guys watching while they smoked. "Looks like our little show down the road has attracted an audience," he said.

"Yeah. I wonder if they're hangers-on from Tedesco's team or if they've already switched allegiance to the new guy."

"If they're still loyal to Tedesco, they won't be around for long."

He shook a cigarette loose from a soft-sided pack of Philip Morris smokes and stuck it between his lips. He offered me one and I waved him off. Then he cranked his window down a crack and lit up. "I've been wondering how you and Frank figured out that your assistant was being held down here."

He put his car in gear and headed downtown.

I turned to face him, not liking the sharp tone now in his voice. "You might've heard that my mother is Diane Black."

"Uh-huh."

"She tipped me off. To save my assistant."

He flicked his eyes at me, then back to the traffic. "Well you see, that's what puzzles me. I'm wondering why she'd do that. The FBI says she's an important Mafia figure with a reputation as a financial expert. And she's also experienced in looking after certain 'personnel' problems."

He turned right onto James Street, heading toward St. Joe's at the foot of the Mountain.

"What's your point? Are you suggesting that Frank and I were doing favours for the Mob? Accepting bribes or some damn thing in exchange for information about my assistant?"

He narrowed his eyes at me. "Now, don't go off half-cocked, Dexter. I just have to be sure of what happened here. It's part of my job to check these things. We've had a few cops over the years who couldn't resist a little palm oil to look the other way."

"Well it sure as hell ain't Frank's way – he's the most honest guy I've ever known. You're barking up the wrong tree, Mister."

He pulled to the curb across from the Medical Arts Building near the hospital and leaned toward me. "Here's the thing, Max. Frank's coming up for promotion soon. And how do you think it would look to the selection board if they found out that one of my men was just a little too cozy with the Mob?"

I stared into his small dark eyes and saw the anxiety of a middle-aged guy who feared he might be putting his pension in jeopardy if he made a wrong move here. "You're not really concerned about Frank's career, are you? You're worried about covering your own ass."

He reached for my arm again and I pulled away.

"C'mon, Max. What I meant was –"

I shook my head and opened the passenger door. "I know damn well what you meant. I'll walk the rest of the way."

He was waiting for me at the entrance to the Emergency ward. "Listen, Max –"

I brushed past him and he didn't follow me in. Then I spotted Frank's wife at the admitting desk. "How's the patient, Angie? What's the doc say about his leg?"

Her eyes were red-rimmed and puffy and she clutched a damp hankie in her shaky hands. "Oh, Max, am I glad to see you. They took Frank up to surgery. I only talked to the doctor for a minute and he told me the bullet has lodged in an awkward spot and it might be difficult to remove. I don't know what that means, but I'm really scared."

She smothered me in a bear-hug and sobbed against my shoulder.

"He's a strong guy, Ange. He's going to recover from this. He'll be chasing you around the kitchen before you know it."

She clutched me tighter. "Oh, my Lord. I hope you're right."

"Where are the twins?"

She released her grip on me and took a step back. "My mother came over. She loves to look after them and she'll spoil them rotten. Now tell me what happened to Frank. They just said you were with him when he was shot."

I led her into the waiting room and we sat beside a Christmas tree covered in cut-out pictures and hand-made cards. A hand-lettered sign said: "Decorations from the Children's Ward". Bing Crosby was singing you-know-what from a hidden speaker and I tuned him out.

I slid my arm around Angie's shoulder. "Isabel was kidnapped by some gangsters so Frank and I were searching for her in an abandoned house where a couple of thugs got the jump on us. Frank was shot right away and I took care of the two guys. I found Isabel tied up in the cellar and after I freed her I called for an ambulance to bring them both here."

She dabbed at her tears with that wet hankie, staring at the brass crucifix hanging on the opposite wall. "He's never been wounded before. I've been dreading this day and it's every bit as bad as I thought it would be." She sobbed again. "No. It's even worse."

I leaned in closer and whispered. "We have to support each other, Angie. Have you seen Isabel yet?"

She jerked back from me. "Did you just say she was kidnapped? I've been so concerned about Frank that it went right over my head. Did they admit her, too?" She tugged my arm, "C'mon, let's find out."

Angie bounced up from her chair, linked her arm through mine and rushed me back to the desk. I inquired about Miss O'Brien from a short, harried nurse whose shift change couldn't come soon enough. She shuffled through some papers and looked up, giving me the cold-eye. "You a relative, Mister?"

"She's my sister," I said with a pretty good quaver in my voice.

Angie raised an eyebrow but remained silent.

"Turn right. Bed four."

Arm-in-arm again, we bustled down the corridor to bed four.

I edged the curtain aside and peered in. Isabel was propped up on a pile of pillows, eyes closed, a green ice-pack at the back of her head. The curtain-rings jangled when I drew the curtain all the way back and her eyes popped open. "Oh, Max. And Angela. How's Frank? Is there any word yet?"

I held up my hand to stop her questions. "You're looking a lot better, Iz."

"I feel better now, and I'm glad to see you both." She spread her arms wide and both of us leaned down to embrace her.

Angie repeated what little she knew of Frank's situation. "Now I'm waiting for news about that operation. It's making me a nervous wreck."

"We'll wait with you," Iz said. "For as long as it takes."

I took Isabel's hand and squeezed it. "What's the verdict on your concussion?"

"I think it's just a big bump. But they want to keep me overnight, just in case."

CHAPTER THIRTY-FOUR

I WAS GROGGY WHEN I awoke the following morning. I'd stayed late at the hospital, waiting with Angela for the result of Frank's operation. We'd left Isabel earlier when the night nurse shooed us out of her cubicle.

It was after midnight when a young surgeon met us in the waiting area on the third floor where Frank had been transferred. "He came through it well," the doc said. "We were able to remove the bullet. But it's too early to tell if his mobility might be compromised."

Angela reached forward and grasped the doctor's hand. "My God, what's that mean?"

"It means he might walk with a limp. That bullet was lodged in his hip near the joint. So we'll just have to wait and see how well he heals."

She leaned back close to me and draped her arm around my shoulder. "Our best friend has a limp, so I'm not worried."

I'd slept in and it was 0930 when I was eating my breakfast and listening to CHML on the radio. A somber news voice intoned, "Even though it's Christmas Eve morning, it seems crime doesn't take a holiday in Hamilton. Police announced this morning that Crime Boss Dominic Tedesco and two of his top lieutenants have apparently disappeared and there's an unconfirmed report that he was spotted at Malton Airport. This comes on the heels of the recent discovery of the body of Salvatore Angotti, formerly of Buffalo, shot and dumped in the Burlington canal. And yesterday, police found three more bodies in an abandoned house on Caroline Street North. All of the dead men had criminal records. A police spokesman said this type of activity often signals a change in command in a crime organization. Also, in a surprising development, police are seeking the whereabouts of a former Hamilton woman thought to have played a key role in these recent gangland slayings. ... In other news ..."

I snapped off the radio and remained at the table, finishing my coffee. An image of that "former Hamilton woman" took shape in my mind – sleek and intelligent.

And a killer.

But when it counted most, she was also a mother who'd helped her son.

I called St. Joe's to learn when I could pick up Isabel, and my call was transferred to the third floor.

"Nurse Magwood speaking."

I stated my business, saying, "I can come and get her at noon."

"No can do, Mr. Dexter. Her doctor wants to see her again before she's released but he's busy all morning. He'll examine her after lunch and if she's okay she'll be discharged about two o'clock. Now, give me your number and I'll let you know."

No damn way I was going to sit around my apartment waiting for this nurse's call. I wanted to be at Iz's side in case that examination revealed anything abnormal. "Thanks," I said. "But I'm on my way now."

At St. Joe's I took the elevator to the third floor and approached the desk, where a tall nurse with auburn hair was on the phone. When she'd finished, she pointed a bony finger at me. "I'll bet you're the anxious Mr. Dexter who can't follow instructions." She raised her hand like a traffic cop. "I know, I know, you have to be with your lady love in her hour of need."

I stared at her, wondering if all nurses were this bossy. Maybe there was a special course for it at nursing school. I leaned forward to check her name-tag. "Guilty as charged, Miss Magwood. Is Miss O'Brien ready now?"

"Not quite." She pointed to a line of chairs along the wall. "Park yourself over there and try to relax. The doctor hasn't seen her yet so I'll call you when I call you."

An hour later, I was returning from the washroom and was surprised to see Iz seated in the waiting room. Her skirt and blouse were rumpled and filthy and her usually neat hair was a tangle of red curls and bandages. But her eyes lit up when she saw me approach and she stood up quickly, then woozied herself back down on her chair.

"Just a bit dizzy," she said. "The doctor told me it might take a day or two to pass. I was so relieved when he said my bump was just a bump. But I needed some stitches where my head was scraped." She extended her arms and I helped her to her feet. "Take me home, Max."

I looked back over my shoulder at Nurse Magwood who was waving us an overzealous goodbye.

Down in the lobby, I called Dave to drive us to Isabel's home. He made more than his usual fuss over her when he saw her weakened state, but after that the busy day-before-Christmas traffic spared us from his usual commentary.

Isabel wrapped her arms around me, her head on my shoulder so she could whisper in my ear. "I'll always be grateful to your mother, Max. She saved my life. And I'm especially glad that you were able to put your unhappy childhood behind you and turn to her for help. I know how difficult it must have been for you."

I'd tilted her chin up and was kissing her when Dave stopped the cab and turned toward us. "Hate to interrupt, folks, but here we are."

He scrambled from his seat and held the door for us. I gripped his free hand in both of mine and gave him a handsome tip. "Merry Christmas, Dave."

It was almost dark outside and beginning to snow when a new Isabel finally emerged from her room: she wore a blue and white University of Toronto football jersey and a pair of blue warm-up pants. She had tried to brush her wavy red hair over the bandage on her head but it stood out as a stark reminder of her ordeal in that dingy basement.

She walked toward me, her arms outstretched, a pair of fluffy white slippers on her feet. Despite her frightening experience she appeared to be relaxed. I sensed that I might've been the first man allowed to see her in her stay-at-home-alone clothes and I was flattered. I pushed up from my chair, my body aching and bruised and took her gingerly in my arms. "We must look like wartime casualties, Iz, but I'm relieved that you're safe and sound. I was afraid that I might've lost the only woman I've truly loved."

She kissed me on both cheeks. "I'd like to hear more of that later, Max. But right now I'm going to fix us a light supper; then we can sit by the tree. I have a little gift for you."

Johnny Mercer and Margaret Whiting were singing "Baby, It's Cold Outside" on the radio as we settled on the sofa beside the tree. I pointed to the snow swirling outside the living room window. "Right on time for a white Christmas."

Her eyes radiated a dreamy glow. "This is nice, Max. I'm beginning to feel human again." She picked up a small bag beside the couch, removed a narrow gift-box wrapped in shiny paper, and presented it to me. Her eyes sparkled as she waited me for to unwrap it.

Way too small for a tie.

I shook it – no sound.

Iz rotated her hand in a hurry-up motion so I ripped off the wrapping, lifted the lid and gaped. "Holy cow! What a beautiful watch."

It was a handsome gold Hamilton wristwatch and when I turned it over I read the inscription, *Love, Isabel* and the date, *12/25/47.*

I took off my well-worn Bulova and replaced it with the Hamilton watch, then held it up so we could admire it. "Looks like a million bucks, Iz. I don't suppose you got it from James Jewellers?"

"Of course, I did. And I met that nice Mr. Suyehiro."

I slipped my hand into my jacket pocket and fingered the box with the earrings from Eaton's. I already knew she had much better earrings and now mine had become a lump of coal compared with this stunning, expensive watch on my left wrist. My gift didn't measure up – and I feared that Max Dexter didn't either. A mile out of my depth was how Frank had put it. And at that moment I believed he was right. Maybe a thousand miles.

Isabel leaned toward me. "What's the matter, Max? You look so glum."

My hand came out of my pocket, revealing the tiny box. "I know it's not worthy of you, it's so small, and –"

She covered my mouth with her lips in a long passionate kiss which left me breathless. "I love you for what you are, Max. Your strength of character, your beliefs, your loyalty. And how you make me feel … you've brought me back to life. And I love you for that most of all."

I flopped back on the couch. Dazed. Speechless. I wanted to jump over the moon.

But she wasn't finished yet; she waved her arm around the room encompassing its plush furnishings. "All of this," she said. "They're just things. I did nothing to earn them. And they mean less to me than a single day with you, Max. When I was bound up and left in that dirty basement I was scared to death that I'd never see you again. I thought about you the entire time and that's what kept my hopes up."

She wagged a long finger at me. "So let's make this the last time we talk about my stuff and my so-called station in life."

"But –"

"No more buts. Now, let's see what's in this cute little box."

I watched the sparkle in her green eyes when she opened the Eaton's box and saw the pearl earrings. "Why, they're lovely, Max. I'll always treasure them because they came from you."

She removed the earrings she was wearing and replaced them with the pearls. "How do they look?"

"Not as good as you do."

She wrapped her arms around me and squeezed. "I've got something else for you." From the small bag beside her she removed another gift-wrapped box about the same size as the one I'd given her.

I glanced at the card. "It's addressed to you, Iz."

"Present it to me. I'll act surprised when I open it."

Sounded odd to me, but what the heck, I was wearing a fancy Hamilton wrist watch.

She opened the tiny box and caught her breath in a dramatic imitation of a starry-eyed chorus girl. "Oh my heavens, it's a ring."

She turned the box toward me.

In it was the largest pearl I'd ever seen. Granted, my experience was almost zilch when it came to jewellery, but this pearl was the grand-daddy of those I'd given her. It was surrounded with a circlet of glistening diamonds. Not just diamond chips, either. This ring might have come from a treasure chest in King Solomon's vault.

It was stunning – I couldn't speak.

Isabel slid closer and snaked her arm around my neck. "It was my mother's engagement ring. She wanted me to have it when I found the right man." She raised her eyebrows and waited.

Sometimes I'm smart.

So I asked her.

END

ACKNOWLEDGEMENTS

At Seraphim Editions: Many thanks to my publisher Maureen Whyte for her steady support of Max Dexter. I'm also grateful to my editor, Bernadette Rule, a smart and savvy writer whose thoughtful comments are much appreciated. And for yet another classy cover, thank you to Julie McNeill of McNeill Design Arts.

Special thanks to Cat London of Catherine London Editorial Services who guided me in the right direction when I wrote myself into another corner.

I'm also indebted to Mob chroniclers James Dubro and Robin F. Rowland for their excellent biography of one of Hamilton's most prominent gangsters: *King of the Mob: Rocco Perri and the Women Who Ran His Rackets* (Penguin Canada, 1987).

I'm grateful for the advice of Stewart Brown, former *Hamilton Spectator* reporter, man-about-town and author of *Brant Inn Memories* (North Shore Publishing, Burlington, ON., 2008), a nostalgic memoir of the famous dance spot. Stew's dad, Gord Brown, a long-time dance band musician and music teacher in the Hamilton area, makes a brief fictitious appearance in this book at Robert's Restaurant.

Thank you to Marion Emo and her staff at the Hamilton Burlington SPCA. Marion was kind enough to provide me with details of the Society's history. She also arranged to refer me to Kevin Degenhard, Chief Inspectorate Officer at the RSPCA in the U.K. who generously shared with me his encyclopedic first-hand knowledge of dog fighting or both sides of the Atlantic.

My on-going thanks to Margaret Houghton, now retired from the Hamilton Public Library, for unlocking many of the secrets of *Vanished Hamilton*.

To our grandchildren whose names have popped up in this series: Grace, Marie, Gillian, Thomas, Trevor and the irrepressible Emma Rose. Yes, along with Max, Dexter and Isabel, that's a total of 9 grandchildren. So far.

To my family and friends whose names are similar to those of the characters in this series – it's fiction, eh?

And finally, thank you to my wife Michèle, my first reader and my eternal flame.

Chris Laing is a native of Hamilton, Ontario. He worked in private business for 20 years before joining the Federal Public Service where he served in the Department of the Secretary of State and National Museums of Canada in Ottawa until his retirement.

Since then he has expanded his longtime interest in detective stories from that of avid reader to writing in this genre. He is the author of the Max Dexter Mystery Series, set in Hamilton in the post-WWII era. The first novel in the series, *A Private Man*, was a finalist for the Arthur Ellis Award, Best First Crime Novel, 2013. The second novel, *A Deadly Venture*, won the Kerry Schooley Award presented by the Hamilton Arts Council in 2015. *A Family Matter* is the third novel in the series.

A collection of his short stories about growing up in Hamilton during WWII, *West End Kid: Tales from the Forties*, was published in 2013 as an e-book only and is available from most on-line retailers.

He now lives in Kingston, Ontario with his wife, artist Michèle LaRose.